Blood in the Dust

Frank Quarternight stood on the veranda of the
Majestic Hotel and looked down the street. It
was saloon after saloon, all the way to the
prairie. He heard music, laughter, a hoot.
John Stone was out there. Sooner or later
he'd find him.

Quarternight placed his hook on the bar.
"Whiskey," he said. The bartender poured the
drink. His hook was clearly visible and several
men knew who he was. His name passed from
lips to ears, and the word spread through the
saloons. Frank Quarternight was in town, and
somebody was going to die. . . .

* * *

**Turn to the back of this book for a preview
of the exciting new Western by Giles Tippette,**

SIXKILLER

SEARCHER

RECKLESS GUNS

Josh Edwards

DIAMOND BOOKS, NEW YORK

RECKLESS GUNS

A Diamond Book / published by arrangement
with the author

PRINTING HISTORY
Diamond edition / May 1992

ISBN: 1-55773-711-8

Diamond Books are published by The Berkley Publishing Group,
200 Madison Avenue, New York, New York 10016.
The name "DIAMOND" and its logo are trademarks
belonging to Charter Communications, Inc.

PRINTED IN THE UNITED STATES OF AMERICA

10 9 8 7 6 5 4 3 2 1

RECKLESS GUNS

1

IT WAS COMMENCEMENT Day at West Point, 1860. Cadets stood stiffly at attention on the parade ground, their leather and brass highly polished. Not a wrinkle showed on their tailored gray and white uniforms, and they wore high hats similar to the shakos of the Prussian Army.

Castellated walls and turreted towers of barracks could be seen in the distance. The mighty Hudson River flowed past the Palisades on its way to the sea. A moderate breeze fluttered flags over the reviewing stand.

Tall, lean John Stone stood ramrod straight in Company D, his eyes on the neck of the cadet in front of him. This was the end of Stone's junior year. Next spring at this time he'd become a second lieutenant in the United States Army, like the seniors graduating that day.

"You are the future of America!" the commandant declared from the podium. "You bear a sacred trust! Your profession is to defend this great nation from its enemies! It is a high calling that we share! It demands our very best!"

The commandant's speech droned on, while threats of war rumbled across America. The North and South had been at each other's throats for twenty years, and the day was approaching when young officers would have to choose sides. The cadets standing in the ranks might soon face each other across the field of battle, with all the fearsome implements of modern war at their disposal.

"The eyes of America are upon you! Your behavior must

be exemplary! The future of the nation depends on you! If we ever meet again, no matter what the circumstances, may we always be good soldiers and good comrades. I salute you!"

The band struck the march, guidons flew into the air. Orders were shouted; the first cadet company moved out in perfect unison, every nuance practiced in hundreds of daily march routines, a smooth, well-oiled machine.

John Stone had arrived at West Point a gangly youth, now was nearly a man. His sword was buckled to his side, his chin strap tight. He'd studied tactics, leadership, weaponry, and yearned for the day he'd command his own troop of cavalry. He hoped to prove worthy of the lofty principles of the United States Military Academy.

Captain Howard of Massachusetts raised his sword in the air, and Company D was off, marching to the beat of drums, stomachs in, chests out, chins down, eyes straight ahead, a man beside a man and a man behind a man, black boots pounding. They performed a flawless column right and proceeded down the runway, legs snapping, fingers straight, sharp young warriors on parade.

The music became louder, a clash of cymbals sent a shiver up Stone's back. He thought, at that moment, nothing could ever stop him. They rounded the far turn, not a man out of position, marching from the hips down, shoulders squared, every heel touching down at the same instant.

They advanced toward the reviewing stand, while America's most distinguished men and women watched the cadets strut their stuff. Stone's blood was hot with pride in himself and his country. The guidons shot up. Every man, at the identical moment, jerked his head to the right.

The cadets looked into the stands, saw senators, congressmen, generals, admirals, important industrialists, pretty young girls wearing their best spring coats. Behind the podium stood the commandant at rigid attention.

"Present *arms*!"

The cadets whapped their outstretched fingers to a point above their right eyebrows, and the commandant saluted back. Stone marched past the grandstand, the music blared. He felt exhilarated; fabulous possibilities stretched before him, he could become a general, senator, engineer, businessman, anything he wanted. He was a member of America's elite, at the pinnacle of his life. His future appeared magnificent, and nothing was too good for him. He raised his eyes above the reviewing stand and looked at the clear blue sky.

It was a beautiful moment, he felt the potential for greatness surging within him. It was hard to imagine he'd soon be plunged into the middle of the bloodiest conflict the world had ever seen.

He lowered his eyes. Something moved on the prairie straight ahead. West Point vanished as he focused on a group of riders heading toward him. If they were Indians . . .

He wore two Colts in crisscrossed gunbelts with the bottoms of the holsters tied to his legs, gunfighter style. A Henry rifle rested in its scabbard, and an Apache knife with an eight-inch blade stuck out of his knee-high black boots. He was six feet two, broad-shouldered, wore an old Confederate cavalry hat. His dark blond beard and hair were long and unruly, after nearly three months on the Chisholm Trail.

The riders drew closer, Stone saw cowboy clothing. They weren't Indians, but could be road agents. Stone wondered whether to make a run for it. Four men, well dressed and barbered, didn't look like outlaws. Their leader raised his hand. "Howdy, stranger!"

They were armed, but soft and pale, spent their time indoors. They pulled their horses to a stop in front of him. The one in front took off his hat and wiped his forehead with the back of his arm.

"Coming up from Texas with a herd?" the man asked.

Stone nodded, watching everybody's hands.

"Name's Jesse Roland. Headed for Abilene? Why don't you come to Sundust instead? It's closer, got better accommodations, here's a list of cattle brokers." Roland handed a sheet of paper to Stone. "They're all reputable men, representing the biggest outfits in the East. I'm a member of the Sundust Businessmen's Association, and we look for the point men of Texas herds, tell 'em about our town."

Stone glanced at the paper. "Never heard of Sundust."

"Less'n a year old. We've got a connecting trunk line to the main railroad farther north, and that makes us twenty miles closer to you than Abilene. Why go the extra distance if you don't have to? We've got everything Abilene has, and more." Roland pointed behind him. "Sundust's thataway. You go to the Blue Devil Saloon on State Street, your first drink's on me. That goes for your men too. Just say my name to the bartender, he'll take good care of you."

A squat man with a hook where his left hand should be crossed the lobby of the Drovers Cottage in Abilene. He was rumpled and bearded, covered with the dust of the trail. Most men in the room figured he was just another cowboy in town for a big blow-out.

He walked up to the room clerk, asked in a low, raspy voice: "Triangle Spur show up yet?"

The room clerk was small and wiry, and the hook excited his morbid curiosity. "Never heard of the Triangle Spur."

"Room for the night."

The clerk placed the register in front of the man, and noticed the oiled holster, mark of the gunfighter. The man wrote his name, and the clerk told him the room number.

The man walked toward the stairs, and the clerk turned the register around. *Frank Quarternight.* Wasn't there a fast gun from Texas by that name?

Quarternight opened the door of his room. The window overlooked the back alley, he glanced at sheds, privies, wood-piles, horses tied to rails. He hadn't shaved or bathed for a week, but was anxious to hit the saloons. He pulled his Smith & Wesson out of its holster, checked the loads deftly with one hand, and reholstered the gun. He strolled toward the door, cigarette dangling from a corner of his mouth. If the Triangle Spur was in town, they'd be in the saloons.

Cassandra Whiteside rode in front of the Triangle Spur herd, atop her palomino mare. She was twenty-four years old, had blond hair, dressed like a cowboy, her hat wide-brimmed, dirty, stained. Strapped to her waist was a Colt in a holster tied to her leg, and in her boot was a knife with a six-inch blade.

She wasn't the same person who'd left San Antone over two months ago. That was a prim lady who never spoke above a whisper, but now she hollered and swore like a man, shot injuns and rustlers, slept on the ground every night, bathed seldom, ate beef and beans at the campfire with the men, wasn't afraid of them anymore.

Abilene was near. The ordeal was almost over. She'd pay

her creditors, begin a new life. The herd spread behind her like a vast brown blanket over the prairie. They numbered twenty-seven hundred mixed longhorns, and she'd started with three thousand in South Texas. Each was worth eight dollars in Texas but twenty-two in Abilene.

She heard hoofbeats. Galloping toward her was Don Emilio Maldonado, the *segundo*. He pulled back his reins, and his wide sombrero hung down his back, suspended from a cord around his throat. He wore a thick black mustache.

"Riders headed this way!" he shouted.

The men passed the word along. Cassandra pulled her rifle out of its scabbard and made sure it was loaded. It might be another of those days.

Cowboys and vaqueros rode forward to join her and Don Emilio. "What's wrong now?" asked Slipchuck, the toothless old ex-stagecoach driver.

Don Emilio pointed straight ahead. "Load your guns, amigos. Sister Death may visit today."

"I'll do the talking," Cassandra said, holding her rifle. "No shooting unless I give the word."

She wished Stone were there, but Don Emilio could lead a fight too. They'd brought the herd across one thousand miles of open country, and weren't stopping now.

The riders came closer, sending up a trail of dust. Cassandra pulled her hat tightly on her head and slanted it to the side, the way Truscott, her former ramrod, wore his. If Truscott were looking down at her from cowboy heaven, he'd say *hold fast and don't take no guff*.

Cassandra sat with her backbone straight and her mouth set in a grim line. The only law on the plains was the law of the fastest gun. The riders numbered fifteen and were led by a young man with silver disks on his hatband and a tin badge on his red and yellow striped shirt. He didn't look more than twenty.

"Who's in charge here?" he asked.

"I am," Cassandra replied.

He looked at her, took off his hat, scratched his head. "A woman. I'll be a son of a bitch."

Don Emilio narrowed his eyes. "What do you want?"

The young man pointed his thumb to the badge on his shirt. "I'm Marshal Buckalew. You owe one dollar fer each head of yer cattle. It's Texas Fever Tariff."

Cassandra heard about self-appointed authorities in Kansas swindling money for the passage of cattle. She looked Buckalew in the eye. "We're not paying any tariff."

Buckalew had blond sideburns and the faint wisp of a mustache on his upper lip. "In that case, turn yer herd around."

"Like hell we will."

He looked at her and smiled. "The little lady talks like a man. You best git out of the way, 'cause somebody's liable to die 'fore this day is much older."

Cassandra didn't reply. Injuns, rustlers, lightning storms, stompedes, no water for long stretches, and this. "Out of our way," she said.

He yanked his gun, and sunlight glinted on the barrel. "I'm a-gonna tell you one last time. The tax is one dollar a head, three thousand dollars in all. Pay up or go back."

"You want a fight," she said, "we'll give you a fight. There are more of you than us, but some of you'll die. You can bet your bottom dollar on that."

"If yer men want to git shot up for a bunch of cows they don't own, it's okay with me."

Don Emilio rode forward. "You are no marshal. Anyone can buy a badge for a few coins. You are a bandito."

"And you're a greaser."

Don Emilio stiffened in his saddle. Buckalew aimed his gun at him. "Say yer prayers."

Buckalew fired, and a hole appeared in the middle of Don Emilio's sombrero. Don Emilio went pale, and Buckalew's riders chortled.

"Are you gonna pay, or are you turnin' back?" Buckalew asked.

The time for talk was over. Cassandra thought she should pay; she didn't want any more killing.

"It's Johnny!" hollered Slipchuck, pointing to a hill in the distance.

They saw a tall, husky cowboy on a black stallion headed toward them.

"Trail boss," Cassandra said. "I'll want to talk with him before we go any further."

"Ain't nothin' to talk about," Buckalew drawled. "He wants lead, we got aplenty."

Stone approached as longhorns stared at him with wide, trusting eyes. He sized up the situation quickly, looked like trouble. The kid with silver on his hat was their leader.

"What's that piece of tin on your pocket?" Stone asked.

"You owe three thousand dollars for the Texas Fever Tariff. Don't pay, go back to Texas. It don't make a shit to me either way."

The grin on Buckalew's face became more pronounced. He'd gotten away with it every time before. Suddenly Stone jumped to the ground and walked toward Buckalew, his scarred leather leggins flapping with every step. Buckalew saw him coming, and made his move.

Stone drew so fast his hand was a blur. A loud booming shot reverberated across the plains. The gun flew out of Buckalew's hand, a cloud of smoke filled the air. Blood oozed out of the hole in Buckalew's hand, an expression of amazement on his face. Stone continued walking toward him, reached up, dragged him out of his saddle, threw him to the ground, pinned him with one hand, pointed his gun between Buckalew's eyes.

"We're not greenhorns," Stone said. "Get the hell out of here."

Buckalew was in shock, teeth chattering with pain. Bleeding and humiliated by a filthy waddie out of nowhere who'd taken him by surprise. The barrel of Stone's gun pressed against Buckalew's nose, bending it around. Buckalew thought his time had come.

"Get on your horse and ride on out of here," Stone said in a deadly voice. "I ever see you again, I'll blow your head off."

Buckalew lay on the ground, stung by the pain in his right hand. The bullet had gone all the way through, and the bleeding wouldn't stop. He pressed his palms to stanch the flow, tried to get up, but Stone kicked him in the butt. Buckalew hit the ground, rolled onto his back. The wound became clogged with dirt and bits of vegetation.

The Triangle Spur cowboys laughed. Buckalew sputtered, his face red with rage. He arose and looked at Stone. "Someday I'll kill you."

"Get on your horse."

Stone aimed his gun at Buckalew, fired a shot. The bullet struck a silver disk on Buckalew's hatband, the hat blew off his head. Buckalew bent to pick it up, and Stone fired again.

The hat danced away. Buckalew made another motion, Stone pulled his trigger. The hat flew into the air.

The chortles grew louder, and Buckalew felt hurt far worse than his wounded hand. "I'd like to remember yer name."

Stone fired, and lead parted Buckalew's hair. "I said get the hell out of here."

Buckalew engraved every feature of the waddie onto his mind. He picked up his hat and placed it on his head, but it looked ridiculous, full of holes, with the brim misshapen. He climbed into his saddle with one hand, looked at Stone one more time, put his spurs to his horse's flanks, and the animal walked away. The assembly of fraudulent lawmen muttered among themselves as they receded into the endless rolling plains.

Slipchuck looked at Stone: "You just made an enemy for life, pard. You ever see that son of a bitch again, grab iron."

Stone turned to Cassandra. "Abilene is two or three days thataway," he told her, pointing to the northwest, "but Sundust is over there, and it's twenty miles closer." He handed her a slip of paper. "List of cattle brokers."

"Never heard of Sundust," she replied, and looked at Slipchuck, old historian of the West. "Ever hear of Sundust?"

"Towns come and go," he replied, "accordin' to where railroad bosses in New York want to lay the next length of track. Never heard of Sundust, but that don't mean it ain't there."

Stone said, "The man told me Sundust was closer and better than Abilene, and he'd buy us all a free drink at the Blue Devil Saloon."

"Somehow," Cassandra replied, "I think our decision should be based on something more than that."

"Did they say anythin' 'bout the whorehouses?" Slipchuck asked.

"I'm sure they'd have anything an old billygoat like you would want," Stone replied.

"What the hell we waitin' fer?"

Cassandra looked at the list of cattle brokers, and recognized big firms from the East. Sundust was two days closer, tomorrow she could take a bath. "Trail boss—point the herd to Sundust!"

Frank Quarternight entered the Alamo Saloon, and old-timers recognized him immediately. There was only one gunfighter who had a hook where his left hand should be. They watched him closely. If he grabbed iron, they'd be first on the floor.

Quarternight saw their eyes in the shadows, acknowledged their silent homage. He made his way to the bar, crowded with cowboys celebrating the end of the months on the trail, everyone talked at the same time. He came to a stop behind a cowboy quaffing a mug of beer. The cowboy felt something sharp dig into his shoulder, turned, saw an iron hook.

"Out of my way," Quarternight growled.

"Just squeeze in, pardner. Bar's crowded as hell."

The cowboy moved to the side, making available a few inches of space, but Quarternight didn't budge. Quarternight gazed into the cowboy's eyes, and the cowboy wouldn't risk his life over a length of wood. He pulled away. Quarternight leaned his ample belly against the bar. "Whiskey."

The bartender saw the hook, stopped what he was doing. Wiping his hands on his apron, he walked toward Quarternight, placed a glass before him, poured whiskey.

"Ever heard of the Triangle Spur?" Quarternight asked.

"Not yet, but if I do, I'll let you know, Mr. Quarternight."

A few heads turned around. The name was well known. Quarternight was aware of the attention, walked to a table against the wall. Men playing poker dropped their cards and stepped away. Quarternight sat and faced the door.

The cardplayers found another table, saloon settled down. Men poured whiskey down their throats, but the atmosphere had changed. Frank Quarternight drank whiskey as news of his presence spread through Abilene.

The cowboys and vaqueros from the Triangle Spur sat around the campfire, eating steak and beans. They'd been dreaming of tomorrow ever since they left San Antone. Whiskey and whores in big feather beds, with chandeliers hanging from the ceilings and big mirrors everywhere. They could taste whiskey on their tongues, and good restaurant-cooked food.

Cassandra sat among them, a cigarette hanging from her lips. Twenty-seven hundred longhorns times twenty-two dollars a head was nearly sixty thousand dollars. She owed nearly twenty thousand, and the rest was hers.

"Boss lady," Slipchuck said, small eyes glittering in the firelight. "Back there in Texas, you said you was a-gonna give us a big party if we got to Abilene, and you'd pay fer all the whiskey we could drink. That go fer Sundust too?"

"Wherever I sell the herd, you boys get your party."

His face broke into a toothless grin. "With all the whiskey we kin drink?"

"You can drink till you're passed out on the floor."

Stone washed his hands in the common basin, dried himself with the common towel. Ephraim, the Negro cook, sat nearby. Their eyes met, but neither said anything. A state of war existed between them, but no one else knew.

Ephraim had been one of Stone's father's slaves, and hated him with deep passion. They'd nearly killed each other in a series of private fist and knife fights in San Antone and up the trail, with no decisive winner. Stone was glad the drive was over, so he wouldn't have to deal with Ephraim anymore.

He filled his tin plate with meat, beans, and biscuits, then sat beside Cassandra. Don Emilio Maldonado leaned against his saddle nearby. "I feel sad," he said. "We have been *compañeros* for so long, sharing work, fighting, even the pleasure of *La Señora*'s companionship. How will we live, without *La Señora*'s beautiful face every morning?"

"Find some other *La Señora*," she said.

"But there is only one *La Señora*."

She looked at Stone, always distant, preoccupied. Sometimes he mumbled military commands in his sleep. Do I really love him?

Frank Quarternight walked into the Lone Star Saloon. Cowboys stared at him in fear and fascination. Everyone got out of his way. "Whiskey."

The bartender poured the glass. Quarternight leaned against the bar. It was the usual filthy frontier whoop and holler. His eyes roved the whores, he'd get one after he shot John Stone. Business before pleasure.

John Stone had shot Frank's brother, Dave Quarternight, one of the fastest guns in South Texas, and Frank had to even the score. It'd be a tough fight, every split second would count. Frank didn't know for sure if he was faster than his brother. Frank had beaten Dave at target practice, and Dave had beat Frank. They were more or less even.

He and his brother had been orphans, parents massacred by Kiowas. A tight bond existed between them, and that damned John Stone shot it to pieces. He didn't know what John Stone looked like, but had a general description. Quarternight hunted men before, only a matter of time.

The Lone Star became silent. Quarternight turned to the door. Tom Smith, Marshal of Abilene, walked toward him, and Quarternight knew it was time for the lecture. Smith wore no visible gun, preferring to subdue troublemakers with his fists, but a Colt was concealed in a leather-lined side pocket, in case of emergency.

Marshal Smith came to a halt in front of Quarternight. "I'll have to ask for your gun."

"Ain't gittin' it."

"I run a safe town. You don't give me that gun of your own free will, I'll take it by force."

Smith moved to get in close, so he could use his fists. Quarternight whipped out his Smith & Wesson. "Hold it right there, Marshal."

"It's against the law to carry a gun in Abilene."

"Tell that to the other men, not me."

"You don't give me that gun, I'll place you under arrest."

"Make a deal with you, Marshal. You got my word I won't use this gun within town limits, unless somebody draws first."

Smith had been looking for a way out of his predicament, now he had it. "Never heard of Frank Quarternight going back on his word," he said. "Plannin' to stay in Abilene long?"

"Leavin' tomorrow mornin'."

"Buy you a drink?"

"We got nothin' to say to each other, lawman."

It was night in the cow camp, and embers of the fire glowed red in the pit. The cowboys unrolled their blankets and smoked their last cigarettes of the day. Everyone was tantalized by Sundust, and were already there in their imaginations, drinking whiskey, fondling whores. Stone met Cassandra on the far side of the chuck wagon.

"You wanted to speak with me?" he asked.

Her golden hair shone in the light of the moon. "I was wondering about us. You haven't said anything, so I thought I'd ask."

"I think we should get married in Sundust," he replied, "then go back to Texas, rebuild your ranch, put together another herd."

She stared at him for a few moments. "Johnny, do you mean it?"

"Wouldn't've said it, if I didn't mean it."

"Do you think you're over Marie?"

He hesitated, and she saw the doubt in his eyes. Marie was Stone's former great love, the bane of her existence.

Stone looked into her eyes. "You're a wonderful woman, Cassandra. Everything a man could want."

"Do you love me the way you loved Marie?"

"More," he replied, because it was expected of him, but deep in his heart he knew he was a liar.

She hugged him, and Slipchuck's head appeared around the edge of the chuck wagon. "Wa'al look what we got here!"

Moose Roykins, former Canadian lumberjack, came behind Slipchuck. "They're at it again."

The rest of the crew gathered near Slipchuck and Roykins. Stone and Cassandra separated.

"Shall I tell them, or will you?" Cassandra said.

Stone faced the cowboys and vaqueros. "I don't know how to say this, so I'll just come out and say it. Cassandra and I are getting married in Sundust, and you're invited to the wedding."

The men'd been expecting this since Stone and Cassandra began sneaking away together back in Texas. "Kiss the bride!" roared Luke Duvall.

"She's not the bride yet," said Stone, "but that won't stop me."

He touched his lips to hers, felt her breasts against his shirt. She was strong and firm, a fine woman. It was time he settled down, and he couldn't do better than Cassandra Whiteside. Love and the promise of new life felt wonderful in his arms, as a nighthawk flew across the face of the moon.

The kid wore a floppy-wide brimmed hat too big for him, and a gun strapped to his waist. His clothes were rags, he had holes in his boots. No one paid attention to him. Another crazy cowpoke.

His eyes fell on Quarternight, and the Texas gunfighter saw him coming. The kid was so young he still had pimples on his cheeks. "Frank Quarternight?"

"That's me."

"Hear you're hot shit with a gun."

Quarternight didn't reply. He thought of the kid shooting cans and bottles on the prairie, preparing for his debut.

"You might be a hot gunslinger," the kid said, "but I bet you don't deserve it no more. You look like just another old drunk to me."

"Boy," Quarternight said, "you don't want to fuck with me."

"I'll draw on you right now, if'n I want to."

"Wouldn't make that mistake, I was you."

"I think you're afraid to fight a man who ain't dead on his feet like you."

"Don't call me afraid, boy."

"Don't call me boy, you old drunk."

"Marshal was in here a while back," Quarternight said, "and I gave him my word I wouldn't shoot no damn fools within town limits, so how'd you like to meet me on the prairie in about an hour?"

The kid turned a shade paler, and he said, "West of town, just beyond the sign—see you in an hour."

"Git outta my face," Quarternight replied, "so's I can finish my whiskey in peace."

Quarternight turned his back, raised the glass to his lips. The kid walked out of the bar, spurs jangling. Quarternight drained his glass and pushed it forward. The bartender uncorked a new bottle.

"Know his name?" the gunfighter asked.

"I'll ask around for you, Mr. Quarternight."

Quarternight sipped the whiskey. Maybe the kid was the next Jesse James, but the odds were against it. Tomorrow the sun would set on his grave.

Cassandra and Stone lay awake beneath their blankets, staring at the starry heavens. Cowboys and vaqueros slept nearby, and the embers were cold in the fire pit.

Cassandra wished she could have John Stone all to herself. She loved him; he'd awakened feelings she didn't know she had. They could make a life together, but Marie still held him in her grasp after all these years and miles.

Cassandra often thought of her phantom rival. She'd seen Marie's daguerreotype, but a picture only shows the outer person. What did she have that made Stone follow her across mountains, rivers, deserts, tractless wastes of prairie, for five years? John Stone was a good man. They had problems, but they'd work them out. Maybe he'd forget Marie after a few kids.

Cassandra's hip touched John Stone, and he felt warmth radiate through him. He'd been thinking about Marie too. Five years of futile pointless meandering search were enough. He didn't want to end up a toothless old drunk in the Last Chance Saloon.

Cassandra was sensible, bright, a hard worker. She wasn't afraid to use a gun. She'd stand by her man. He couldn't go wrong.

Yet he couldn't forget Marie. He'd loved her since he was six. They'd shared everything. Where was she? Why didn't she wait for him after the war ended? Was she dead? Had she gone insane?

He'd arrived home after Appomattox, found her gone. Some said she went West with a Union officer. He'd hunted her ever since, asking the same questions, but no answers. Drifting aimlessly turned him into a drunkard. If he didn't settle down, he'd end up in a gutter. Cassandra was a good woman. He couldn't give her up for a fading memory.

Stone felt her beside him, and couldn't resist such a delicacy. He rolled over, their lips touched, they pressed against each other. His fingers sought the buttons on her shirt.

"Don't wake up the others," she whispered.

Men stood in bunches, smoking cigarettes, drinking whiskey out of bottles. The sign said:

WELCOME TO ABILENE
CATTLE CAPITAL OF THE WORLD

The lights of Abilene sparkled in the distance. Bets were running ten to one in favor of Quarternight. The young man checked and rechecked his gun. He practiced a few fast draws at imaginary opponents. His name was Shelby, and he rode drag for the Circle B.

Quarternight approached on the road, boot heels crunching gravel. They watched the famous gunfighter walk to the far end of the dueling ground, where the moon shone over his shoulder.

"Whenever you're ready, boy," Quarternight said, the legs of his baggy pants spread apart.

"I told you ter stop callin' me boy."

"Only one way you can make me do that, boy."

"Let's git it on, old man."

Quarternight lowered his right hand to a position above his gun. He had chubby jowls, and his belly hung over his belt. Shelby, young and slim, was poised like a cat to strike.

A terrible shriek rent the night. A young woman struggled to break through a cordon of men. "Don't let him kill Billy!"

"Hush now!" said one of the men sternly. "This ain't no place for a woman!"

She was a skinny wraith who thought she was grown. Her teeth were bared, lightning in her eyes. "Please stop them, sir! He can't kill a boy!"

Quarternight looked at Shelby. "You still got time. Nobody'll think the less of you if you walked away. I killed more men than you got years. I got no beef with you."

"I don't walk away," Shelby said, feeling rattlesnake energy radiating from the plains. If he killed Quarternight, he'd be famous. Never ride the drag again.

The young woman tried to break loose from the men. "Stop them!"

"Ready when you are," said Shelby to Quarternight.

Quarternight measured distances. He was a professional, nothing haphazard. Tensing for the final spring, he said, "You're the one who wants this fight, so make yer move, boy."

The young woman shrieked, the kid's hand dropped to his gun. Quarternight pulled his trigger, his Smith & Wesson fired, and a split second later Shelby's gun went off. A bullet struck the ground near Quarternight's toe. The young woman sounded like a banshee gone insane. Shelby had an expression of surprise on his face. A trickle of blood appeared at the corner of his mouth, his eyes glazed over. He staggered, and the gun fell out of his hand. He turned to Quarternight, whispered something unintelligible, then his legs gave out. He went crashing to the ground.

Quarternight holstered his gun. His hand didn't have the speed of ten years ago, or even five years ago. If Shelby had been a hair faster . . .

Quarternight looked at the young man on the ground. Maybe, on another night, Shelby would've been faster, and Quarternight dead meat on the ground. Quarternight knew he was losing his edge gradually as he got older. One of these days, in some godforsaken town, Death would be waiting.

They turned the girl loose. She ran, face streaked with tears, toward the body of her lover, fell on top of him, pressed her cheek against his bloody face, called his name pathetically, her body wracked with sobs. Quarternight headed toward his horse. A victory celebration was waiting for him, and maybe a whore. He climbed into his saddle and rode toward the famous saloons of Abilene, their lights flickering like beacons in the star-spangled night.

2

A RED SLIVER of dawn lay on the horizon. Cassandra and her men devoured beef and biscuits washed down with thick black coffee. Sundust lay straight ahead, but one problem remained. What would they do with the former *segundo*?

He'd been *segundo* before Don Emilio, his name was Braswell. Something terrible had happened to him in Texas. His face was purple and his mind was destroyed.

Cassandra shuddered when she thought about it. He'd been the nastiest cowboy in the bunch, argued and fought with everyone, and even had threatened Cassandra. One morning they found him dead in his blankets, no apparent cause. They buried him, rode away, heard his cries, dug him up. Now he communicated in grunts, followed orders, but had no will of his own. Everyone thought Ephraim had something to do with it, because Braswell had been especially abusive toward him, but no one had any proof. Were the people of Sundust ready for the former *segundo*?

She washed her tin plate in the bucket. The men broke camp for the last time on the trail. Tomorrow night they'd be in Sundust, except for the ones on night duty. She walked toward Don Emilio.

"You're in charge until I return," she said. "Move the herd as close to town as you can. Send one of your men in to tell us where you are, understand?"

He wore his sombrero, and a shock of black hair hung over

17

his forehead. "Señora, please do not marry John Stone. He is a good man, but not for you. I should not speak, but my heart pushes me forward. You deserve someone who loves you more than he."

"I forbid you to mention the subject of marriage to me again." She turned abruptly, walked toward her horse. Don Emilio watched the sway of her hips. She was his golden goddess, and he'd lost her. Somebody slapped his shoulder. Don Emilio looked up and saw John Stone.

"Don't take it so hard. You know how women are. There's no figuring them out."

"You don't love her, and you know it."

"You and I've been around for a long distance, amigo. Love is where you find it. There are many flowers on the prairie, and if you don't get one, there are always a hundred more."

"Not for me," Don Emilio said bitterly.

"You think you love Cassandra, but you'd leave her just as you've left all the others."

"You are a gringo. You could not possibly understand."

"Life is a game of cards, and you play the hand you're dealt. I'm getting married, amigo. Can't you wish me well?"

"Good luck," Don Emilio said without conviction.

They shook hands. Don Emilio gazed longingly at Cassandra atop her palomino mare. Stone climbed onto his horse, and Don Emilio walked toward the remuda. The Triangle Spur prepared for the final push to the railhead in Sundust, end of the long hard drive.

Frank Quarternight sat by the window in his hotel room, whiskey in his hand. He glanced toward the bed, saw the whore take off her clothes. Her skin was white as the sheets, and her ribs visible through her skin.

"Come over here," she said, breasts standing firmly, eighteen years old.

He was ashamed to take off his clothes and let her see his loose flesh. She'd rather be with a young man, but he'd killed one tonight. He unbuttoned his shirt.

"What you want first?" she asked.

He stepped out of his pants and felt her eyes upon his naked folds of blubber. Quickly he crawled beneath the covers. His head swam as it hit the pillow.

"You all right?" she asked.

"Let me close my eyes for a few moments."

She held his face, he snored softly. *Older men are like children in a candy store,* she mused. *They want everything in sight, but can only handle very little.*

She sipped her whiskey, while the famous gunfighter slept like a baby in her arms.

Stone and Cassandra came to a sign that said:

SUNDUST
Cattle Capital of the Plains
One mile to Go
Don't give up Now

They spurred their horses, and the animals could smell manure in the stockyards, smoke, the garbage dump, open outhouses, gunpowder.

"I know sometimes a man can say things he later regrets," Cassandra told Stone. "I've lived with your moods the past few months, and they run all over the place. You want to change your mind, don't be afraid to say so."

He glanced at her sharply. "You trying to back out of it?"

"I just want to give you all the rein you want."

"Sounds like you want to give me so much rein, I won't even be in sight."

"I don't want a man who'd rather be someplace else."

"When I tell a woman I'm going to marry her, it's not something I just dreamed up. You're the woman for me."

They saw Sundust, a scattering of shacks on a vast plain. Railroad tracks and stockyards lay beside it, with a curved column of smoke arising from the smokestack of the engine car.

"Don't get too drunk, Johnny," she said. "I don't mind you having a few, but let's not pass out on any floors, all right?"

"Anything you say."

Acres of holding pens were packed with snorting cattle, their long journey nearly over. Hereafter they'd ride boxcars, and next stop was a slaughterhouse. The stink of cow manure, urine, and dust filled the air as cowboys loaded cattle into the cars. Engineers sat in the cabs of their locomotives, watching the show.

Cassandra and John Stone turned onto the main street of Sundust. The first building on the near corner was a saloon, across the street was another saloon, and there was a saloon every few doors down. They heard the tinkle of pianos and women's laughter. Somebody fired a shot. A group of cowboys galloped down the street, screaming at the tops of their lungs. Cassandra and Stone pulled their horses to the side so the cowboys could pass.

Stone peered through the door of the nearest saloon, and saw men sitting at the bar, cowboy hats silhouetted by rear windows.

"Looks like you can't wait," Cassandra said. "Don't let me hold you back."

"I'll see you to your hotel."

"I can get there myself."

"Let's understand something, Cassandra. I'm a good-timing man and I never tried to hide it. You marry me, you've got someone who appreciates a fine glass of whiskey."

"Wouldn't mind if it were just one."

"Sometimes it's a man's sacred duty to get drunk."

"Getting drunk isn't duty. It's the mark of a pig."

"Oink," said Stone.

"Stop that."

"Oink oink."

They came to the Majestic Hotel, a big box three stories high, with a wide veranda in front.

"Getting a room for the both of us?" Stone asked.

"Not until we're married."

"We've been married since that night in Texas, you know the one I'm talking about."

"I want a church ceremony. This lady doesn't get married every day."

"Give me the addresss, I'll be there in my best clothes, on time every time."

"I don't know why I love you so much, but I do." She kissed his bearded cheek. "Stay out of trouble, all right?"

She entered the lobby of the Majestic Hotel, crowded with men in every conceivable manner of dress. All eyes turned toward her, and the old whoremasters among them raised their brows, because this was an exceptional female creature.

It wasn't the sheer of her cheek or the curve of her hips, nor her piercing blue eyes or pronounced cheekbones. Her most arresting quality was strapped to her slim waist: a Colt in a well-worn holster. They seldom saw a woman heeled like a man.

The room clerk looked at her, and even he was impressed. Women appeared in the Majestic Hotel all the time: whores, wives, sisters, and mothers. Some had been scared, and many left after one look around the lobby. A few walked in as if they owned the place. This one carried a gun, and looked like she knew how to use it.

She was tall and looked tawny underneath her rough trail clothes. Her legs were slightly bowed from so many days on horses, and she appeared ready to wrestle a steer to the ground. Her beauty was striking, without a smidgeon of makeup, only the dust of the trail. There was nothing dainty about her.

"Room for the night," she said.

"One person?"

Cassandra looked at him, and he was shorter than she, with a round face and carefully waxed mustaches, a different species of animal compared to her rough sons of bitches back with the herd. They could tear the Majestic Hotel apart in fifteen minutes. "Yes, and I'd also like to have a bath."

The clerk pushed the register toward her. Cassandra took the pen in hand, and the clerk could see hard calluses, the scar near her right thumb, no wedding ring. She signed her name and pushed the register back.

"What herd you with, ma'am?"

"Triangle Spur."

The clerk wrote it on the registration form, handed her the key. "Hope you enjoy your stay with us, Miss Whiteside."

"Mrs. Whiteside."

"Will your husband be joining you?"

"I'm a widow."

"If you require anything, Mrs. Whiteside, please don't hesitate to ask."

"I'd like to buy some new clothes. Where would you recommend?"

"You might try Shaeffer's Dry Goods a few doors down. They have everything a lady might want."

No store can give a lady everything she wants, Cassandra thought. She carried her bedroll to the second floor, entered her room, saw whitewashed plank walls, bed, chair, and atop the desk a printed list of authorized cattle buyers. *Authorized by whom?* she wondered.

She threw her bedroll in the corner, washed her face and hands in the basin. The bed would be her first in nearly three months, but there was work to do. She needed clothes. A person can't conduct important business in rags.

She looked at herself in the mirror and tilted her hat low over her eyes, the way Truscott always did. He'd been her foreman, big brother, father, uncle, and sometimes she'd felt strange desires. Trampled to death in the worst stompede of the drive, and she couldn't forget him. The man had been utterly fearless, tough as rawhide.

The sooner she sold her herd, the better she'd feel. Her cowboys and vaqueros were chomping their bits, they hadn't seen a town since Texas.

It was midafternoon, the street of Sundust full of riders, carriages, wagons. Rows of horses were hitched to rails, sidewalks crowded. She looked like a cowboy at first glance, if you didn't examine too closely. She saw the sign: SHAEFFER'S DRY GOODS.

It was a wooden box like the Majestic Hotel, one story high. Dresses and pants hung from the rafters. A man, a woman, and children worked behind the counter. Cassandra took off her gloves and tucked them into her gunbelt the way Truscott always did. She found an empty spot at the counter, and a little girl popped up her head in front of her.

"Help you, sir?"

"I'd like to buy a pair of pants, a shirt, and a hat," Cassandra said out of the corner of her mouth, because that's the way Truscott always had talked.

The child was eight years old. "Are you a man or are you a woman?"

"Woman."

"Ever use that gun?"

"Please get me the clothes. I'm in a hurry."

A man with a mustache appeared beside the little girl. "I'll take the gentleman, Annabelle."

"It's not a gentleman, Daddy. It's a lady."

Mr. Shaeffer's eyes scanned Cassandra's face. "Sorry, ma'am. Can I help you?"

Cassandra told him the items she wanted, and he retrieved the merchandise from boxes. She tried on a new pearl-gray cowboy hat.

"Perfume?" he asked.

"Your best."

He reached behind him, plucked a small bottle from a box, pulled the cork, let her sniff. It reminded her of New Orleans, where she was born and raised. "I'll take it."

"Traveling with a herd, ma'am?" he asked.

"Triangle Spur," she replied, dropping coins on the counter. "You meet any cattle buyers, you tell them I've got nearly three thousand head of the finest longhorns God made."

"*You* came all the way up the trail, ma'am?"

"That's right," she said, lifting the pile of clothing. "I'll be staying at the Majestic Hotel, anybody wants to talk business."

John Stone made his way toward the Blue Devil Saloon. They'd promised him a free drink there, his decision was easy. Out of all the variegated saloons in Sundust, he sauntered toward its swinging doors, stepped out of the backlight. It was a long narrow room shaped like a coffin with the bar on the right, tables on the left, dance floor and stage in back. Above the bar hung an oil painting six feet wide, naked harem girls taking baths in a palace garden pool.

Their odalisque eyes followed Stone as he crossed the saloon, passing tables crowded with men arguing, gambling, reading old newspapers, swilling rotgut. A few solitary ones with drool in their beards stared vacantly into space. Stone came to the bar and looked at the row of bottles on the shelf below the mirror.

This was his first saloon since Texas, and his mouth watered at the sight of amber liquid in shiny bottles. "Jesse Roland said he'd buy me a whiskey if I came here."

The bartender poured the drink. "What herd you with?"

"Triangle Spur. Lots of cattle buyers in town?"

"More'n you could shake a stick at. You got cattle to sell, you won't have 'em long."

Stone looked at the whiskey, and it called to him from its lucid depths. If he were smart, he'd leave it alone. But nobody ever called him smart. *I can handle a few drinks. Not that goddamned weak.*

He raised the glass, let a few drops trickle onto his tongue. It had the deep smoky taste of charred barrel. There was nothing like a drink of whiskey to brace a man. He tossed the entire contents down his throat.

It hit him like a bolt of lightning. For a few seconds it sizzled his innards, then the warm glow came on. He pushed the glass forward. "Hit me again."

"What part of South Carolina you from?"

"How can you tell I'm from South Carolina?"

"Hear lots of accents. Can pick 'em out."

Stone reached into his saddlebags, took out the dented and bent photograph of Marie. "Ever see this woman?"

"Don't believe I have."

Stone stared at the picture of the pretty young blonde who resembled Cassandra Whiteside. *Where are you?* He spotted an empty table near the dance floor, walked toward it, passed a whore leaning against the bar.

"Need a gal he'p you drink that whiskey, cowboy?" She followed him to the table, dropped to the chair opposite him, seventeen, tooth missing in front. Her red hair was fixed in spit curls on her forehead, and her breastworks were pitiful. Yet she was pretty, a naughty little girl.

"I'm Sally Mae."

"John Stone."

"Just hit town?"

"Yes, thank God."

"I came a year ago, when we all lived in tents. Been paid yet? How's about a drink?"

"You've got more money in your garter than I have in my pockets, saddlebags, and blanket roll. Why don't you buy one for me?"

She smiled and wagged her finger in front of him. "It don't work that way, cowboy."

She walked away. Stone leaned back in his chair. Many nights on the trail, riding night duty with the herd, he'd dreamed of the next saloon, and here it was in all its splendor.

Numerous panes of glass had been broken out of the windows and replaced with old barn boards. Tables and chairs leaned crookedly on a planked floor covered with cigarette butts, spit, splatters of whiskey, broken glass, chicken bones, and somebody's boot. Legs of the furniture were stained with gooey tobacco juice. Bullet holes were visible on the walls. Names badly spelled were carved into tabletops, but the feeling was there.

The dirt-stained mirror behind the bar had been witness to every conceivable drunken orgy, marathon poker games, shootouts, knifings, eye gougings, earlobes bitten off, broken bottles, slashed faces, and every other incredible excess and act of brutal violence. You could smell meanness in the air.

The cuspidor near Stone's table was filled with a liquid so vile as to defy analysis. The floor surrounding the cuspidor was covered with brown gunk, because many cowboys, under the influence of strong rotgut whiskey, couldn't see straight. The bar rail was covered with scars, and at the end hung a gob of a man's hair left over from the last brawl.

The beat-up old lantern on the wall—how many scenes had it illuminated? Maybe it came from a miner's tent, sodbuster's hut, outlaw's hideout, but it couldn't illuminate the minds of men blind drunk.

Everybody packed a knife and a gun, and a man could bet, on any given night, somebody's going to die.

Dark, dingy, filled with spit, vomit, and urine, it was an oasis for cowboys, and they talked of nothing else on the trail. This filthy dark hole in the wall represented their highest aspirations.

In the painting above the bar, Nubian slaves carried water to naked ladies glistening forever in the sunlight. Stone lowered his eyes to the whores. Hungry girls scrambling to stay alive. The life wore them out and beat them down. Garish cosmetics covered pale sickly skin never seeing the light of day. Disease ran rampant among them. The only romance most cowboys ever knew was with these poor lost creatures who charged the going rate for their kisses and hugs.

A boy dropped a sheet of paper on Stone's table. Another list of cattle buyers, his eyes lazily glanced down the names. Then he blinked, brought the paper closer. "You know this Lewton Rooney?" he asked the bartender.

"Comes here all the time."

"About my age, this tall." Stone held out his hand.

"I'd say so."

Stone looked stunned. "Know where I can find him?"

"Prob'ly in his office this time of day."

• • •

Cassandra's hair was combed, tanned skin scrubbed clean, new cowboy clothes not too big for her. She slanted her fine new cowboy hat on her head Truscott style, and left the room.

It was late afternoon when she stepped onto the veranda of the Majestic Hotel. The air was filled with soot and dust, one saloon after another. Cowboys staggered in the muddy street, some passed out on benches in front of business establishments. The shooting usually started after ten at night in San Antone. She hoped John Stone wasn't drunk yet.

She searched for the office of a cattle broker, saw a white church with a steeple. The sign above the front door said:

MOUNT ZION CHURCH OF GOD
Bean Supper
Saturday Night

Cassandra didn't need beans, but a prayer of thanks was in order. She opened the door, ahead was the altar. Nailed to the wall were two crude branches in the form of the cross.

She removed her hat, and freshly shampooed blond tresses fell out, cascading to her shoulders. She sidestepped into a pew, dropped to her knees, clasped her hands together.

Thank you, Lord, for my safe arrival. She saw the open plains, herd spread over hundreds of acres, faces of men who'd fallen along the way, fighting for cattle that didn't even belong to them. They rode for the brand, and died for the brand.

She whispered their names: Joe Little Bear, Calvin Blakemore, Duke Truscott. She saw Truscott walking bowlegged toward her, his leggins flapping in the breeze. He'd loved her in his rough cowboy way, she knew that now, and would never forget him. Sometimes she felt his spirit hovering above like a guardian angel.

"You all right, miss?" The kindly, crinkly old face of a minister with a white collar. "Reverend Phineas Blasingame, at your service." He bowed, showing neatly parted white hair.

She brushed the tear away. "I was saying a prayer for friends of mine who died recently."

"They are with the Father in heaven, so you needn't worry about them. I don't believe I've ever seen you before . . ."

"Cassandra Whiteside, Triangle Spur."

"You look a little piqued, my dear. Care to have a cup of tea with an old preacher?"

"I have an awful lot to do."

"We can pray together in the rectory for your departed friends. You say you've just arrived from Texas?"

"About two hours ago."

"You traveled with your husband, I assume?"

"I'm a widow."

He gazed at her with new interest, his eyes flicked up and down her figure. "Tea is a marvelous restorative," he said. "You've come a long way."

He led her through a long, dark passageway to a small room with chairs around a low, circular coffee table. A stained-glass window showed Jesus as a child, studying the word of God.

"Must've been quite an adventure," he said, "coming up the trail with a crew of cowboys. Not many women do it. Do you own your herd free and clear?"

"Yes, and I'm looking for a reputable cattle dealer. Can you recommend someone?"

A grotesquely misshapen creature entered the room, carrying a tray with a pot of tea and two cups. It was a woman four feet tall, with a massive hunch askew on her back. Two holes were her nose, and her lips were twisted into a smile and snarl.

She served the tea and backed out of the room. Reverend Blasingame spooned sugar into his tea. "Name's Emma," he explained. "A beggar when I met her, not a very good one. Close to death, in point of fact, but I knew Christ wouldn't turn his back on her. She's been with me ever since, and maybe she disturbs some people, but that's all right with me. You were saying before you wanted to know the name of a reputable cattle broker? Well, let me tell you, you're smart to be cautious. More swindlers and thieves in Sundust than you could shake a stick at. Never saw such a sinkhole of depravity in all my days, but it gives me strength to know there are young women like you who revere the Lord. In my opinion, the most honorable and dependable cattle broker in Sundust is Dexter Collingswood, churchgoer, model citizen, town alderman, father, husband, I could go on and on. His office is on State Street, next to the bank. I'd recommend you see him immediately."

"There's one more thing I'd like to ask, Reverend Blasingame. I'm planning to get married while I'm in Sundust. Could we have the service here?"

"No reason why you shouldn't. Who's the lucky gentleman?"

"My trail boss."

"Known him long?"

"About three months."

"How long's your husband been dead."

She cleared her throat. "About three months."

He made a gentle smile. "I'd be happy to marry you. Have to speak with the groom first, make sure he intends to lead a solid Christian life, and raise his children in a God-fearing home."

"My husband-to-be isn't a regular churchgoer," she told him, "but he's a decent man. I don't think the Lord would turn him away."

Little Emma hurried into the room and whispered something into Reverend Blasingame's ear. Reverend Blasingame cleared his throat. "A poor unfortunate woman is dying of an incurable disease, and I must visit her now. Will you excuse me, Mrs. Whiteside?" He clasped her hand warmly. "Mr. Collingswood's office is next to the bank."

Reverend Blasingame watched her go from the shadows in the corridor, stroking his pink chin with his fingers. She was a rich young blossom, and perhaps he could become her pastor. With a sardonic chuckle, he made his way to his office, sat at his desk, opened a drawer. He poured liquid from a brown bottle into the glass, then filled it with water. The small brown bottle was labeled "Tincture of Laudanum," a derivative of opium. He drained the glass, returned it to the drawer, slammed it shut.

There was a knock on the door. Tod Buckalew entered the office, his right hand bandaged. "Dad . . . ?" he said.

Reverend Blasingame raised his finger to his lips. He didn't want anybody to know they were father and son. "What happened to your hand?"

"Got shot." Buckalew dropped heavily onto the sofa. "My gunhand too."

"Somebody beat you to the draw?" Reverend Blasingame asked with disbelief.

"Came at me out of nowhere before I was set. It was a fluke."

"Be set every moment, my boy. I'm surprised at you. Who did this?"

"John Stone. Trail boss for the Triangle Spur. Big ugly son of a bitch."

Reverend Blasingame touched his finger to his chin and looked pensive for a few moments. "Big spread?"

"Three thousand head, I'd say. Wouldn't pay."

"You've got to kill this John Stone, otherwise no one else'll pay the tariff either. Practice with your left hand. God didn't give you the gift just in one hand."

"Why'd God let me get shot?"

Reverend Blasingame's eyes gleamed beneath bushy lashes as he leaned toward his son. "Because of your sins, my boy. Have you ever turned your back on the poor? Do you indulge in dirty practices? I know you go to the cribs."

Buckalew was embarrassed, looked at his bandaged paw.

"You can't do anything without me knowing," Blasingame said. "You'd be surprised at how fast a man will betray his brother, never mind a total stranger." He smiled, placed his hand on his son's shoulder. "I can understand how you become lonely sometimes. I'm sure God will forgive you. But understand, not even God can help you when you let another man get the drop on you. Lie low for a few days, practice with your left hand." Reverend Blasingame kissed his son. "Come back when you're well, and I'll have something for you to do, all right?"

It was a small clapboard shack on the edge of town, and the sign on the door said:

Captain Lewton Rooney
District Representative
Boston Beef Shippers

Lew Rooney had commanded Troop F in the old Hampton Brigade, but Stone knew him even before that. They'd been classmates at West Point, lived across the hall from each other in the dormitory.

Stone raised his hand, held it in midair. What if Rooney were busy? Stone stepped to the side and glanced through the curtains. A man behind a desk faced another seated on a chair. Both noticed Stone, he jumped back. There was a shot, the pane of glass broke, and Stone yanked his Colt.

The door flew open, two men carrying guns rushed outside. One had a pug nose and freckles, wore a suit, looked Irish. Stone's Colt nearly fell out of his hand.

The other man was elderly, dressed like a cowboy. "What in tarnation's goin' on here?"

Nobody spoke. Stone and the freckled man stared at each other for a few moments.

"I don't believe it," Stone said.

Lewton Rooney turned to the third man. "I'm afraid something important has come up, Mr. Bennington. Can you come back later, say tomorrow, around noon?"

"We're in the middle of a deal, Rooney. This ain't time to stop."

Rooney raised a forefinger. "On the contrary, it might be the very best time to take stock, so we understand what we're doing. You've got two thousand head of fine steers there, Mr. Bennington, and you've brought them a long way. A deal like this is nothing to rush into."

Bennington's brow furrowed with thought. "Maybe you're right. Tomorrow morning toward noon?"

"I'll be waiting."

Bennington walked away. Stone and Rooney stared at each other, and the years rolled back. Each saw a young West Point cadet, sword buckled to his side.

"How long's it been?" Rooney asked.

"Since we were mustered out, I reckon."

There was silence for a few seconds as they looked each other up and down. "Still wearing your old campaign hat, I see," Rooney said. "Mine fell to pieces long ago."

Stone took off his hat and looked at it. It was stained and worn, but still held its shape. "Long as it gives good service, I won't throw it away."

"Good for a free drink every now and then, I suppose."

"Less often than you might think."

"We ought to have one right now."

"You won't get any argument from me."

Stone followed Rooney into the house. Hanging on the wall was Rooney's commission as a second lieutenant in the Army of the Confederacy. A framed photograph of Bobby Lee was nailed nearby. Rooney had gained weight, premature lines engraved his cheeks. He wore a cravat and clean white shirt, his suit draped perfectly over his body as he poured two glasses full of whiskey.

"To all good soldiers," Rooney said, raising his glass.

They drank, sat opposite each other. Stone looked at the Confederate flag hanging on the far wall, Confederate cavalry sword mounted over the bookcase.

"Still fighting the war?" Stone asked.

Rooney was embarrassed. "Doesn't hurt business when I point out I wore gray, like most cowboys in Texas. A man's got to get along."

"I'll drink to that."

Rooney refilled the glasses. "You look like you just hit town."

"I'm trail boss for the Triangle Spur, believe it or not."

"Sold your herd yet?"

"Nope."

Rooney winked. "I'd appreciate your business, as we say."

"I'll tell the boss lady."

"My prices are competitive. I aim to please. Have another drink?"

"Don't mind if I do."

They'd fought together, drunk together, chased girls together, and lent each other money. They'd been through good times and bad times. If you've ever fought beside a man, there's a special bond. But somehow it wasn't the same.

Rooney cleared his throat. "Guess you think I've sold out."

"Don't think that at all."

"Captain Lewton Rooney working for the Yankee invader, just another whore."

"We're all whores one way or the other, and there's no more Yankee invader. You said you're not fighting the war anymore. Neither am I. If somebody from Boston offered me a good job, I'd take it."

"You mean that?"

"I truly do."

"Let's have another drink."

Rooney poured two more glasses. They looked at each other down the years. Each saw a young lieutenant riding into battle with yellow sash flying, cannons firing, air full of Yankee bullets.

"Them were the days," Rooney said. "How could anybody dream it'd come to this? I'm a commission man, and you're a . . . cowboy?"

"I've held every rotten job you can imagine, and they tried to hang me in one little town. I'll tell you a funny thing: yesterday I was thinking about you. I remembered the commencement parade when we were juniors. You ever think of it?"

"From time to time. We all thought we'd be great men someday, what a joke. The war took the best out of me, I'm afraid." He shook his head sadly. "I'm not the man I used to be."

"You got your own house, don't look like you're starving, got whiskey, and nobody's shooting at you. Count your blessings, my friend. Could be a lot worse."

"You know what I'm talking about."

"I've just come up the trail with the Triangle Spur. If you're bored, I suggest you try it sometime. We were hit by Osage, Comanches, and a gang of rustlers. It wasn't Gettysburg, but close as you'd want to get."

"Sounds better'n being a commission man."

"I don't see you tied to that desk. You can walk out of this room right now. You want to be a cowboy, be a cowboy. Look at me. I've never been in better physical condition."

Stone rolled up his shirt and showed a bulging tanned bicep muscle. Rooney pulled back his sleeve, and it was flab like the belly of a fish.

"Make you a proposition," Stone said. "You come to Texas with me, and you can work for the Triangle Spur. Thirty dollars a month, and your chuck. It's not nearly what you're getting now, but you'd be outdoors on the hurricane deck of a horse, and you wouldn't have to tell folks: 'I'd appreciate your business.' We've got a good crew, a good cook, although he's slightly bonkers, and we don't take guff from anybody." He pulled his gun. "This is the only thing that matters in Texas."

Rooney saw a dark rangy cowboy with a beard and a look in his eye that said watch out. Rooney lowered his eyes to his own tailor-made suit, the perfect crease on each pant leg, the proper amount of white cuff showing. John Stone was a wild man, and he'd become a commission man.

"I've got a good life here," Rooney said. "Things keep going the way they have, I'll have my own brokerage, and that can make a man rich."

"A man wants to work in an office all day, it's okay with me. Do you remember, back at the Point, sometimes at night we'd slip away, go to a tavern?"

"We sure got pissed."

Stone leaned forward, a wild glint in his eyes. "Let's do it again, right now, you and me, just like the old days. Drink until our pockets are empty, and if anybody starts anything, too bad for them. Maybe we can even see some dancing girls."

"I know just the place."

They drained their glasses, put on their hats, moved swiftly toward the door.

3

REVEREND BLASINGAME WALKED down the main street of Sundust, carrying his Bible. "Good evening, Mrs. Riley," he said, touching his cane to his flat-brimmed black hat. *Another three months, I'll have your farm.*

The good pastor saw a forlorn girl of sixteen on a corner. "Heard your mother's doing poorly?"

"Doctor says she don't have long to live, Reverend."

"I'll visit her later, and we'll pray together. Need money?"

"Bank's got us by the throat. We're borrowed to the hilt."

Reverend Blasingame handed her some coins, and several pedestrians saw the transaction. How typical of the kindly old holy man, always giving of himself. The young girl stared at the money in her palm.

"The Lord will bless you for this, Reverend."

"He already has, with your lovely smile."

She blushed, and he continued on his way. Her family had a fine stretch of bottomland, and when the old lady croaked, it would become another of Reverend Blasingame's secret holdings.

Across the street on the second floor above the Sagebrush Saloon was the Lipscomb County Farmers Association, Reverend Blasingame's main enemies. They wanted Sundust to be the hub of an agricultural area, not the den of wickedness for wild, inebriated Texas cowboys, but there wasn't enough money in farming to suit Reverend Blasingame. One good

35

gambling saloon running full tilt could earn more in a night than the average farm earned in a year. All the farms in the area were in trouble, and that's why Reverend Blasingame was able to buy them for next to nothing.

A group of sporting ladies approached. Reverend Blasingame maintained his saintly composure, though once he'd frolicked with them in the rectory.

"Evening, Reverend," the girls said, smiling flirtatiously.

Reverend Blasingame tipped his hat. "May the Lord bless and keep you, ladies."

They passed, pretty in their tawdry way, but Cassandra Whiteside was a woman of quality and great beauty. A whore sells herself to the highest bidder, but a woman like Cassandra Whiteside had to be broken like a wild mustang.

He came to a sign:

DEXTER COLLINGSWOOD
Cattle Broker
Highest Prices Paid

Reverend Blasingame opened the door. A clerk sat behind a desk, scratching pen against paper.

"I want to see Mr. Collingswood, if he's available," Reverend Blasingame said.

The clerk opened the door. Reverend Blasingame entered the office. Behind the desk sat a man with a large, sharp-featured face, piercing eyes, a wart on his nose. "Surprised to see you here, Reverend. Thought you didn't want it known we're hooked together."

"I speak with everybody in this town from the lowest beggar to the most distinguished business leaders. If Christ could consort with tax collectors, can I not have a word with one of our foremost cattle brokers?"

Collingswood smiled, but it looked like a grimace. "Have a seat, Reverend. Get you something to drink?"

"Coffee, if you please." Reverend Blasingame laid his Bible on his lap. "A woman will be coming to see you shortly, name of Cassandra Whiteside. She's a widow with a herd of three thousand mixed longhorns. Get it at the best price, but don't give her the money. I'll handle that end, understand?"

"What's so special about this one?"

"Do as I say, and bear in mind that I want this deal. Lose it, and I'll lose you."

It was dark in the office. Shadows etched deep lines on Reverend Blasingame's face, and his eyes glowed red-hot coals. Collingswood knew of the reverend's hired guns, led by kill-crazy Buckalew. "What if another broker highballs me?"

"Highball him back. What we lose on the apples, we make up on the potatoes. Just get her name on the contract, there'll be a bonus for you. I don't think you'll have any competition. I recommended you to her, and she'll do as I say."

Collingswood smiled, one brow raised. "A fine God-fearing woman, eh, Reverend?"

Reverend Blasingame winked. "The best kind."

Buckalew rode across a flat plain, beneath the cloudless sky. He drooped in his saddle, worst day of his life. Gunhand bandaged and stiff with pain. Any two-bit kid could kill him. Hide like an animal.

He came to the lee of a hill, climbed down from his horse, pulled the saddle off. He hobbled the horse, unrolled his blanket. No fire, unless he wanted arrows and tomahawks for breakfast. He opened his saddlebags, took out a slab of roast beef.

He cut a slice and placed it in his mouth. Dry, no mashed potatoes or gravy. If it hadn't been for John Stone, he'd be in Sundust living like a king.

His daddy wouldn't acknowledge him in public, but took care of him fine on the side. Daddy was a great man. Buckalew felt he'd let him down.

He finished his meal, nothing to do except sleep. He sprawled on the ground, resting his head on his saddle. In the distance a prairie dog shrieked, caught suddenly in the talons of a hawk. He wished he could have someone with him, but trusted nobody except his father.

His momma never told him who his daddy was, till she was on her deathbed. Then she let the secret out of the bag, said ask him for help.

Buckalew found Blasingame in Denver. At first the preacher pretended not to know what Buckalew was talking about, but grew more interested when he learned Buckalew was a fast gun. Since then they'd got along perfectly. He led the gang that enforced his father's deals, lived high off the hog. The only requirement was keep his mouth shut about who his daddy was.

His daddy was the only one who understood him. He'd disappointed him today, but would shine in his eyes again, after he shot John Stone.

I'll just wing him at first, then shoot pieces off'n him, watch him die.

Cassandra entered Collingswood's office, the cattle broker rose behind his desk. Her grip was solid. Collingswood examined her tanned complexion and sun-bleached hair.

"Reverend Blasingame gave me your name," she said. "I own a herd of mixed longhorns, my count is twenty-seven hundred. They fed out in the Nation, are in first-class condition. It's my understanding they're worth twenty-two dollars a head here at the railroad."

"Prime steers might fetch twenty-two dollars a head, but mixed cattle aren't worth nearly that much. The market has been down lately."

Cassandra had been counting on twenty-two. "What price do you think I can expect?"

"Have to look at the herd. Tomorrow morning be all right?"

"Can't you give me an estimate for mixed longhorns in first-class condition? Prices won't fluctuate between now and tomorrow morning, will they?"

The smile froze on Collingswood's face. He wasn't used to being pressured by women. "Mrs. Whiteside, I'm not quoting a price on cattle until I inspect them with my own eyes. It's good business."

"Can't even take a shot at it?"

She irritated him, but his boss ordered him to make the deal. "All I can tell you, Mrs. Whiteside, is I'll beat any other broker's legitimate price, but I emphasize the word 'legitimate.' Sundust is full of crooks, just like Abilene and every other cowtown. It's important to deal with a reputable broker."

"I'll be here first thing in the morning with my trail boss," she replied.

* * *

Frank Quarternight walked to the front desk of the Drovers Cottage in Abilene. All eyes were on him. "Checkin' out," he said.

The clerk handed him the bill. Quarternight reached into his pocket for the money when a handful of coins dropped onto the counter. A gambler stood beside them.

"Allow me," he said.

Quarternight looked at him. "I slept in the room—I'll pay for it."

"No offense . . ."

Quarternight hoisted his bedroll to his shoulder, held it steady with his hook. His gunhand was empty and loose as he moved toward the door. Gentlemen tipped their hats, and some of the ladies gave him that forthright look. Everybody wanted the kiss of death, but nobody wanted to die.

He crossed the veranda, it was a cool autumn night. His horse was tied to the rail, saddled and ready to go. He walked toward the horse when somebody suddenly shouted: "Watch out!"

Quarternight went for his gun. A bullet zipped through a corner of his bedroll, and he saw a figure with a rifle. He grit his teeth and fired. The figure jerked, and the rifle shot a bullet into the sky. Quarternight triggered again, and gunsmoke billowed around the sidewalk.

He sucked wind when he saw Shelby's skinny girlfriend stagger to the side, trying to fire the rifle again. He should gun her down, but hesitated. He'd never shot a woman before.

She dropped the rifle and looked at him through half-closed eyes. Blood dripped from her nostrils and soaked the front of her calico dress. Her knees gave out, she collapsed onto the ground. Townspeople gathered around. "Get the doc!"

Quarternight holstered his gun. She'd loved the kid so much she took on a dangerous gunfighter. It was difficult for him to comprehend. Marshal Tom Smith pushed through the crowd, spotted Quarternight. "What happened?"

"Tried to bushwhack me."

A man kneeled beside her. "No need to wake up the doctor," he said. "She's dead as she'll ever get. Anybody know her?"

Nobody said a word. She and her man were drifters. Potters Field. Four men carried her corpse to the undertaker, blood dripped from her hair onto State Street. Quarternight tied his blanket roll behind his saddle.

Marshal Smith said, "Mr. Quarternight—it's nothin' personal, but we'd appreciate if you don't come back to Abilene. Killin' always happens when a man like you's around."

"Don't go where I'm not wanted," Quarternight said, " 'less'n I have business."

He climbed into the saddle and rode his horse into the middle of the street. Cowboys, gamblers, and ladies lined the sidewalk, watched him pass. His horse trudged through the center of town, and Quarternight felt troubled. He didn't mind killing men, but not a poor scraggly girl. Ashes were on his tongue as he disappeared into the darkness at the edge of town, headed south toward his next appointment with destiny.

John Stone and Lewton Rooney drank at a dark corner of the Blue Devil Saloon. At the next table, a spirited game of poker was being played.

"Ever run into anybody from the old brigade?" Rooney asked.

"Met one of my sergeants in Tucson not long ago," Stone replied. "He was still in the cavalry. We sang the old anthem together."

Stone and Rooney looked at each other.

"Should we?" asked Rooney.

"Why in hell not?"

They opened their mouths and roared the lively hard-driving tempo of Jeb Stuart's favorite song:

> *"If you want to smell hell, boys*
> *jine the cavalry . . . "*

They pounded their fists on the table, and it was like the good old days. The poker game continued without hesitation, and the song blended into the overall racket of a saloon packed with men hollering at the tops of their lungs.

"I'll order two more," Rooney said. "Don't worry about money. I've got plenty for all of us."

Rooney called a waitress, and it was like West Point again. They shared what they had, nobody kept accounts. Rooney rolled a cigarette.

"Ever think about Ashley?"

There was silence for a few moments, then Stone said, "Sometimes."

"How about Beau?"

"Beau who?"

"Beau Talbott. You, Beau, and Ashley were like brothers. Don't tell me you've forgotten Beau."

"Haven't forgotten him."

Stone grew up with Ashley Tredegar and Beau Talbott, all three went to West Point. Ashley commanded Troop C, and the Yankees shot him out of his saddle at Yellow Tavern.

"To Ashley," Stone said.

They raised their glasses. A cowboy whooped at the next table and wrapped his arms around the pot he'd just won, a cigar sticking out of his teeth.

"Wonder what happened to old Beau," Rooney said. "Heard he came west too."

Stone said nothing.

"You all right?" Rooney asked.

"What makes you think I'm not?"

"Your face just did something funny."

Stone sipped whiskey.

"You ever hear anything about Beau?"

There was silence for a few moments. Stone looked toward the bar.

"Just asked you a question," Rooney said.

Stone reached into his pocket and took out his bag of tobacco.

"I say something wrong?"

Stone lit the cigarette, blew smoke out the side of his mouth. "Beau's dead."

"How do you know?"

Stone took another drink of whiskey. A swarm of bees buzzed around his head. "I killed him."

A queer expression came over Rooney's face. "You're serious?"

"It was him or me."

"I thought you were friends."

"He turned outlaw. Tried to shoot me, but I got him first. Rather not talk about Beau anymore."

Silence returned to the table. Stone had buried Beau at dawn on the desert near Santa Fe. His two closest boyhood friends were gone. He raised his glass, a bright colorful figure suddenly appeared in front of him. Stone went for his gun.

A painted clown in baggy pants held out his hand. "Don't shoot, pardner," he said in a squeaky voice. Then he placed a leaflet on the table. "See you later, at the carnival."

The clown moved away from the table. For a moment Stone thought he was one drink over the line. He read the leaflet:

CARNIVAL
Welcome One and All
Games Freaks Dancing Girls
Free Prizes

"Carnival arrived this morning," Rooney explained. "Pitched tents on the other end of town. We can go over later, if you want."

Stone gazed at Rooney, and the years fell away. Whenever Wade Hampton's officers met, Stone had seen Rooney. They'd been through hell together. "The world turns upside down," Stone said, "our heroes have feet of clay, but not Bobby Lee. I still think he was a great man, and I'm proud I served under him."

"Grant sits at the rich man's table," Rooney replied, "while Bobby Lee is president of a little college nobody ever heard of. If I had a son, I'd rather he went there than West Point."

A cowboy smashed another over the head with a bottle, shards of glass flew through the air. A brawl broke out near the bar. Rooney looked at Stone and saw the captain of the lacrosse team, a member of the fencing team. "We all thought you'd be the first to make general," Rooney said.

"General disaster, maybe."

"Whatever happened to that girl you were going to marry, the pretty blonde—what was her name?"

"Marie. I returned home after the war, she'd disappeared. That's what I'm doing out here. I've been looking for her all across this goddamned country." Stone's mind fuzzed out for a moment, his brain soaked with alcohol. "What are we talking about?"

"Marie."

"I gave up on her. Now I'm marrying somebody else. The strange thing is she looks an awful lot like Marie."

"Does she dress like a cowboy?"

"How do you know?"

A tall blond woman wearing a six-gun walked among the tables. Stone got to his feet and waved. She headed toward him.

"I thought I'd find you in one of these filthy disgusting places," she said to Stone. "How drunk are you?"

Stone's eyes were nearly closed, and one shoulder was raised higher than the other. "Dear," he said thickly, "I'd like to present an old friend of mine: Captain Lewton Rooney. Lew, this is my bride-to-be, Cassandra Whiteside."

"The resemblance is amazing," Rooney said.

Cassandra knew who he was talking about. "You knew Marie?"

"Yes, ma'am."

"I'd like to find out more about this woman whom I resemble so much."

"Uncanny," Rooney replied.

Stone was seriously drunk, she realized with dismay. This wasn't her range-hardened trail boss, but a saloon rat. Truscott had been the same way. They were good men, but something serious was wrong with their minds.

Stone pressed his lips against her cheek. "What you been up to?"

She didn't like the smell of whiskey, and wrinkled her pretty nose. "While you've been celebrating with Captain Rooney, I've attended to business. Tomorrow morning you and I are scheduled to show the herd to a broker, but I don't know if you'll be able to make it."

"I'll make it," Stone said thickly. "Stop drinking after this one. Then we'll go to the Majestic Hotel and turn in, all right?"

Rooney interjected: "I'm a cattle buyer myself, and I'd appreciate your business."

Cassandra recalled what Reverend Blasingame told her about crooked cattle buyers. Rooney was as drunk as Stone, and she didn't want to do business with a drunk. "I've already begun negotiations with one buyer. If a deal isn't made, I'll keep you in mind."

"Who's the buyer?" Rooney asked.

"Dexter Collingswood."

Rooney groaned. "He's the biggest crook in town."

"He was recommended highly by Reverend Blasingame."

"That old fraud? He owns most of this town. We call him Reverend Real Estate."

"But he's a minister, a man of God."

"Between sermons he conducts business like everyone else. If he steered you toward Collingswood, he's getting a piece of the deal. Old Reverend Real Estate doesn't do anything unless it pays off."

"Didn't seem that way to me," Cassandra replied. "I received quite the opposite impression."

"He gives a helluva sermon," Rooney said, "and he sure knows his Scripture, but those of us who've been here since the beginning know what he is. There's talk he even owns the bank."

"Are you sure he's done all these things? He seems like a sweet old pastor. Do you have proof?"

"Reverend Real Estate never puts his name on paper."

The ash from his cigar fell into his glass of whiskey. His eyes were bloodshot and the front of his suit had become stained. Was the allegation of such a man worth taking seriously?

"What would you pay for twenty-seven hundred head of mixed longhorns in first-class condition?" Cassandra asked.

"Twenty dollars a head."

"You couldn't go to twenty-two?"

"Have to take a look at the cattle. If they're exceptional, I might up the ante."

A chorus of boos and whistles spread across the Blue Devil Saloon, as two men carrying guitars walked to the stage. A cowboy near the bar, with an Indian scalp hanging from his belt, cupped his hands around his mouth and hollered: "We don't want no broke down geetar pickers! Where's the girls?"

A cheer went up at the mere mention of the word. The two men stood on the stage, dressed like cowboys except for the red silk bandanna around the neck of the one on the left, and the gold piping on the black shirt of his partner.

"Evening, gennelman!" said red bandanna. "I know you'd

druther have dancin' girls, and so would I, but they're comin' on later. Right now you got us, and we're the Prairie Troubadours. My name's Chet, and this here's Sam."

A chorus of snarls and growls arose from alcohol-lubricated throats across the length and breadth of the saloon. "Git off the stage! We want the gals!"

"We damn shore ain't gals," Chet said. "We're just a couple of old geetar men." He looked at Dave, they strummed, the saloon filled with twangy chords. The Prairie Troubadours opened their mouths:

> *"Way down in South Texas*
> *Where the Rio Grande flows*
> *Where cattle is a-grazin'*
> *And the cactus grows*
> *'Twas there I attended*
> *The Cowboys Halloween Ball . . ."*

Every cattle crew had somebody who could plunk a guitar or blow a mouth organ, but the Prairie Troubadours were exceptional musicians. They sang of the open range, horses, steers, and the girls they left behind. There was something rough about them, they'd roped and branded too. The life they sang of was their own, and they knew it in the fibers and sinews of their bodies.

> *"When we left the ranch*
> *the sun was high*
> *had the best trail boss*
> *money could buy . . ."*

Cassandra looked at her trail boss. His eyes were sleepy, and a cigarette dangled out the corner of his mouth. This wasn't the man who'd thrown a gunfighter to the ground yesterday and threatened to blow his brains out. If John Stone was a drunkard now, what would he be in five years?

At the Mount Zion Church of God, several supplicants knelt in the pews. A candle flickered on the altar, making the cross jump and twist on the wall. The door to the church never closed, so the faithful could use the facilities whenever the spirit moved them. The poor box near the door was locked, because Reverend Blasingame knew well the wickedness in the hearts of the children of Eve.

A grotesque figure approached the poor box, key in hand. It was Little Emma, dragging her club foot behind her. She dropped to one knee, unlocked the poor box, emptied its contents into a basket. Then she carried the basket to the back of the church, disappeared behind the altar, passed through the dark corridor, knocked on a door.

"Come in?"

She shuffled to Blasingame's desk. "Poor box," she croaked.

"Good girl." He patted her head. "Bring me a sandwich, will you?"

Reverend Blasingame upended the basket, spilling coins onto the desk. Looked like a good haul. He sorted the coins and placed them in piles. The donation box usually was good for at least ten dollars a day, but now, with so many cattle crews in town, it amounted to nearly twenty. He wondered if the take could be increased with a new sign:

Help the Families
of Cowboys Who Died on the Trail

He wrote the words on a piece of paper. Every cowboy had lost a friend on a drive. It could be even bigger than his candle concession. Tomorrow he'd give it to a sign maker.

There was a knock on the door. "Come in."

Collingswood entered the room and removed his derby. "Thought you might want to know the Whiteside woman dropped by."

Reverend Blasingame turned to him. "And?"

"She'll be a tough nut to crack."

"I want that herd. Price is no object. Go as high as you have to."

"She wants twenty-two dollars a head."

"Pay it."

"Mixed longhorns aren't worth that much."

"I said pay it."

Collingswood made a lopsided grin. "It doesn't matter what number we put on the contract, eh, Reverend? She won't see a penny anyway."

"You're getting the picture."

"Sure is a looker, but she's suspicious."

"Makes the game more fun. When'll the deal go down?"

"Supposed to look at the herd tomorrow, with her trail boss. He might be a problem."

"I'll handle him. Just give me her name on the dotted line."

Collingswood winked. "Can I have some of her when you're finished, like we did with the Sully woman?"

The Prairie Troubadours plucked the last notes of their song, and the saloon exploded with applause. Cowboys rushed forward and carried the musicians off the stage, propelled them to the bar.

"Nothin' like an appreciative audience," said Chet, reaching for the closest glass. He touched glasses with Sam, and they knocked the first ones back.

Rooney raised his hand, but the waitresses were busy elsewhere. Cassandra realized it was getting late. She looked at Stone. "Have you checked into the hotel yet?"

"Why can't I spend the night in your room?"

"Not till we're married. We've returned to civilization, and should act accordingly." She wasn't anxious to go to bed with a drunk who hadn't bathed for a week.

A hand dropped on Stone's shoulder. He looked up and saw the smiling toothless face of Slipchuck. Next to Slipchuck stood stern Don Emilio, and behind them were three of the most dangerous vaqueros from the Triangle Spur.

Don Emilio bowed to Cassandra and cleared his throat. "Señora, we have moved the herd to a stream a few hours from here. All is well, I am happy to say."

"Who'd you leave in charge?"

"Duvall."

Either Don Emilio or Stone should be with the herd, but they played by their own rules. "Return to the herd, Don Emilio. Take these men with you."

The vaqueros mumbled angrily, they wanted to stay and get drunk. Slipchuck was so distressed he spat on the floor.

"The herd hasn't been sold yet," Cassandra explained, "and I don't have much money. I can't pay you a penny till somebody buys the cattle."

Rooney leaned forward, light from the lantern dancing across his features. "Be happy to buy every man from the Triangle Spur a drink."

Slipchuck and the vaqueros cheered. The waitress bought glasses and a bottle. Ventilation was so poor, Cassandra nearly choked from the stench. Don Emilio sat beside her.

"I trust you have been well, Señora?"

She looked at her *segundo*, a former rancher himself, the vaqueros had been his top hands. "You don't need to worry about me, Don Emilio. I can take care of myself."

"Many desperadoes in these places." He looked at Stone sprawled in his chair. "I do not think the trail boss would be much help if there was trouble."

Stone whipped out his gun and pointed it at Don Emilio's nose so fast it made Don Emilio blink. "Don't ever count me out, amigo."

"*La Señora* is depending on you, and you can barely keep your eyes open."

"I've never let the boss lady down, and I never will."

Don Emilio turned to Cassandra. "Is this the man you are going to marry? Look at him. He is a disgrace."

Cassandra couldn't disagree. Her rough and ready trail boss was slumped in his chair as if he didn't have an ounce of strength left in his body.

The vaqueros fell into a tug of war over the bottle, and Don Emilio shouted in Spanish. They stopped fighting immediately. Don Emilio took the bottle in his hand. "There is a lady present," he said. "Next man who misbehaves will die."

He placed the bottle in the center of the table, and no one made a move. Slipchuck cleared his throat, reached long bony fingers toward the bottle. He poured himself a drink, then politely passed the bottle to Manolo, one of Don Emilio's most lethal vaqueros. "*Gracias,*" said Manolo with a polite smile.

The bottle passed from man to man, and Cassandra couldn't leave now. The men would think she didn't want to sit with them; they were extremely sensitive beneath their tough hides. If she didn't keep them in line, there was no end to the mischief they could do.

"Anybody know what these whores charge?" Slipchuck asked, eyeing a dark-haired dove who appeared part squaw.

There they go again, Cassandra thought. *Their favorite subject.*

Don Emilio cleared his throat. Slipchuck realized he'd said the wrong thing.

"Find out myself, soon's I git paid," he muttered, raising his glass.

Stone looked at Don Emilio. "You're not drinking, amigo?"

"Do you see whiskey in my hand, *borrachín?*"

"Since when did you stop drinking?"

"A long time."

"Can't be that long. Last time I saw you in San Antone, you could barely stand."

"How could you see, since you were passed out underneath the table?"

"You're not fooling anybody, amigo. You're not drinking because you know *La Señora* doesn't like it. If she did like it, you'd drink by the barrel. You're in love with *La Señora,* and you'd do anything she says, like a trained dog. But get one thing through your head: I'm marrying this woman, and you're wasting your time."

"She will be unhappy for the rest of her life," Don Emilio said.

"You're as big a drunkard as I am, but you're holding off to impress *La Señora.*"

"Are you saying I am a liar?"

"Don't have to say it,'cause you just did."

Both men rose from their chairs.

"That's enough!" Cassandra shouted.

Their hands froze in midair and they glared at each other over the top of the table.

"Sit down and behave yourselves!"

They dropped to their chairs and continued scowling.

"If *La Señora* were not here," Don Emilio said, "you would be in hell now."

"Anytime," Stone said in a deadly tone of voice.

"Men are beasts," Cassandra replied. The entire crew had been fighting among themselves all the way up the trail.

Don Emilio replied, "He called me a liar. I will kill him."

"He's pretending not to be a drunkard," Stone said, "so you can be his next conquest. Don Emilio falls in love all the time, you see. Today he'll kiss your hand, tomorrow he'll kiss some other woman's hand. He knows I'm telling the truth, that's what makes him mad."

Don Emilio said sincerely, "Señora, I admit I have not lived the life of a priest. I have been with many women, but I was only searching for the one love of my life. Now I have found you. It would not bother me so much if John Stone were a smart man, like a doctor or lawyer, or he owned a big ranch. I would even surrender you to a bald-headed professor who wears glasses on his nose, because a professor at least knows something, but it hurts me to know you would prefer a worthless no-good *borrachín* to me. He will ruin your life— mark my words."

Reverend Blasingame sat behind his desk, eating apple pie. Food stimulated his mind, and he schemed grand designs. A great metropolis would rise out of the plains, and he would control it from the finest cathedral in the world.

Dirt farmers were flies in the ointment. They fenced off open range to keep out herds from Texas. They'd flushed many a cattle town down the drain, and he couldn't let that happen to Sundust. He wasn't getting any younger, and it was time to reap the rewards for years of dedication to the Holy One.

The door opened, Runge walked in. Slim as a snake, with a short blond beard, he said, "You wanted to see me, sir?"

"Have a seat."

Runge's eyes danced excitedly, and he looked like a trapped rat. He sat on a chair and didn't know what to do with his legs.

"I believe you were there when Buckalew was shot in the hand," Reverend Blasingame said. "He'll be out of action for a while, so I'm placing you in charge of the boys. There's something I want you to do. Some cowboys are in town from the Triangle Spur. Take the boys and beat the shit out of them. You should probably shoot one, to make the point. Understand?"

Runge looked as though he were going to jump out of his skin. "What point?"

"They should get out of Sundust, and never come back. You do a good job, you could end up in charge permanently. We don't know how long Buckalew will be out of action." Reverend Blasingame tapped the back of his hand against Runge's shirt. "Think you're as fast as Buckalew?"

"Don't know."

"You wouldn't be afraid of him?"

"I ain't afraid of nobody."

"Good for you. Gather up the boys and do what I told you."

"Might take a while to round 'em up. Reckon most of 'em's at the carnival."

"Carnivals are sinkholes of depravity," Reverend Blasingame said. "Hootchy-kootchy dancers and flimflam men. I tell you, watch out for carnivals. The devil's playground, I call them."

A nervous smile came over Runge's face. "You just told me to kill somebody, but you think carnivals are bad?"

"I do the work of the Lord. Pray upon it, and we'll discuss the matter further next time we meet."

Blasingame ate apple pie. Success was made of many tiny steps, and next was Cassandra Whiteside. "She won't be so high and mighty when her cowboys are scared out of town," he muttered. "I'll end up with her herd, for which I'll pay exactly nothing, and she'll be eating out of my hand."

4

FRANK QUARTERNIGHT SLUMPED in his saddle as his horse trod the endless rolling plains. Stars twinkled above, a crescent moon hung near the horizon. The night was filled with the buzz and chatter of insects, and a bird shrieked.

Quarternight slept, awoke, and slept again. He'd been dozing since departing Abilene, slipping in and out of dark and bloody dreams about Shelby and his girl.

No one had ever loved him the way that scraggly bitch loved Shelby, he wondered what it felt like. Sure would give a man confidence, and maybe it's what pushed Shelby into dangerous territory.

The only women Quarternight slept with were whores. Maybe it was his belly, but he'd seen men with bellies bigger than his, and beautiful wives too. They knew something, he hadn't a glimmer of what it was. Maybe women were afraid of him. Thank God for whores.

Reverend Blasingame walked past the saloon district, crossed the tracks. He came to the side of town where decent people lived.

"Lovely night, isn't it?" he asked, tipping his hat. *Screwed him out of the Bar Z.* "Good evening, Mrs. Applewhite. Good to see you up and around again." *Got her farm in my desk drawer.* "God be with you, Mrs. Blakely." *High and mighty now, but when I get my hands on her boardinghouse, she'll do anything I say.*

He saw something dark lying near the base of a cottonwood tree. "Oh, my Lord," he said. "It's a bird." He lifted the quivering feathered creature tenderly as a crowd gathered. "I believe its wing has broken. The poor little thing."

He held the bird for them to see, an expression of deep solicitude on his face. One wing was out of whack, and dried blood matted its feathers.

"Maybe Dr. Wimberly can do something," Reverend Blasingame said, holding the bird like a precious crystal treasure. He ran on his little legs down the street, accompanied by the others. They arrived at Dr. Wimberly's door, knocked loudly. It was opened by the doctor, dark bushy eyebrows.

Reverend Blasingame thrust the bird toward him. Dr. Wimberly led them into his office. Somebody moved the lantern closer. Reverend Blasingame felt the bird's heart beating. "Now, now," he said, stroking the bird's head with his finger.

Dr. Wimberly examined the bird as Reverend Blasingame wrung his hands in anguish. The bird was terrified of the heavy-footed giants crowded around and nearly died of a heart attack.

"Only a little break," Dr. Wimberly said. "Should be fine in a couple of weeks, unless something inside is broken, but I don't think so." He filled a basin with water and washed the bird's wound.

"Guess you don't need me any longer," Reverend Blasingame said. "I'll take care of the bill."

"No bill for you, Reverend. Let's say it's a little something I did for the Lord."

"God bless you, brother."

Reverend Blasingame walked out of the doctor's office, and there was silence for a few moments.

"People can say what they want about Reverend Blasingame," Mrs. Hudspeth said, "but they don't know him the way we do. Did you ever, in your life, see such love and consideration for a poor helpless creature? Now there's a man who lives the Christian life!"

"He sure knows his Scripture," asserted Mrs. Applewhite, whose farm was in Reverend Blasingame's desk drawer.

He paused by the door, listening to their remarks. Then he silently walked away, his face wreathed with a beatific smile.

He circled around and came to the back door of a small cottage near the edge of town. He knocked three times on the door.

It was opened by Abigail Thornton, the town's schoolmarm. "You look like the cat that ate the mouse," she said. "What happened?"

"Ran into some people—my assistance was required. Miss me?"

She was a gangly woman with saucer eyes, snaggled teeth, early forties, and she led him through the kitchen, down a hallway, up the stairs.

They'd didn't light the lamp in the bedroom, because Abigail didn't want her neighbors to guess she might be there with Reverend Blasingame. The lamp in her parlor was aglow instead, so neighbors would think they were studying Scripture together. They undressed in the darkness, bony schoolmarm and porky parson, then crawled beneath the covers. The room filled with pants and sighs, the cat came in to look. Reverend Real Estate was buried between the schoolmarm's legs, she chewed an old rag to muffle her screams of joy.

John Stone's head lay on the table, eyes closed, mouth hanging open. Every other man at the table was drunk except for Don Emilio, who sat erectly in his chair, his eyes burning into Cassandra. The Blue Devil Saloon had become even more crowded and raucous than before.

She hadn't intended to stay so late, but she'd never been in a saloon before; it had all the fascination of a zoo. At the bar stood a man whose clothing would be appropriate on the floor of the New York Stock Exchange, while lying on the bar rail beside him was the most filthy dismal drunken cowboy imaginable.

The whores horrified her. She worried about ending up like them someday. All she had was the herd, and she'd need a man who could help her, not drag her down. Her eyes fell on John Stone, unconscious on the other side of the table. "Don't be too hard on him," said Rooney, one arm thrown over the back of his chair, gazing at her through half-closed eyes. "Johnny's been in bad spots. I could tell you stories, raise the hair on your head. Can you imagine what it's like to walk over a battlefield after the shooting's ended, and you can't put your foot down anywhere except on a dead man, or part of a dead man?"

Cassandra saw a landscape covered with soldiers, some in blue, others gray, entwined forever in the cold embrace of death.

"Johnny lost his best friends," Rooney continued, "and never got over it. He was nearly killed himself. You can't judge him as you judge other men. Some veterans are better at covering it up than others, but Johnny's honest, he doesn't hold anything back."

Cassandra was touched by Rooney's remarks. She placed her hand on his. "You're a good friend."

"He was a helluva soldier, let me tell you. His men would follow him anywhere. Very few of them survived the war, and Johnny feels responsible."

Don Emilio said, "Señor, no one here is judging John Stone as a man. We have seen his courage many times, and do not doubt his skill as an army officer. But *La Señora* is planning to marry him, and that is a horse of a different breed. Does she want a husband who is like this all the time? We are sorry so many of his friends have died in the war, but that is no reason to marry him." He looked imploringly at Cassandra. "I am a drinking man myself. I love to get drunk—I admit it. But I am not drinking now. My love for you is stronger than my love for drink. Evidently our friend here does not feel the same way."

Could she deal with Stone drunk on a regular basis? Nothing more disgusting than a drunk, and some of them were dangerous when angry.

"Amazing, the resemblance," Rooney said to her. "You and Marie could be twins. She was quite a beauty, just like you."

"How did she behave? Was she smart?"

"I'd say clever rather than smart. Very good manners. Perfect lady."

"Did you like her?"

"We were all in love with her, but she only cared for Johnny."

"I think he's still in love with her. Why do you suppose she left without leaving a note or message for him?"

Rooney looked at Stone to make sure he was asleep. "Sherman's Army passed through the county where she lived. The courthouse was burned to the ground. Records were destroyed. Many civilians were killed, and I think she was one of them."

Runge entered the Blue Devil Saloon, followed by Reverend Real Estate's personal army of street brawlers and gunfighters. They'd been gathered from the back alleys and robbers roosts of the frontier, and would rather punch a man in the mouth than plow a row of corn or brand a steer.

They broke through cordons of drunken cowboys, made their way to the bar. Runge placed one foot on the rail.

"Triangle Spur here?" he asked the bartender.

"Over there." The bartender pointed a bottle at the table where Cassandra and her men sat.

Runge didn't expect a blond woman in cowboy's clothes, but orders were orders. He wanted to impress the old man with his ability to get the job done.

"Wipe 'em out," he said.

Sometimes they had to shoot people, other times burned property, this was the part they liked best: kicking ass. Runge hooked his thumbs in his gunbelt and walked toward the Triangle Spur.

"We want this table," he said.

All heads resting on the surface began to rise. Stone blinked his eyes and tried to clear the cobwebs out of his brain. Runge signaled to his men, and they charged.

The Triangle Spur cowboys arose from the table, and Runge's men collided with them. A cowboy in a green shirt threw a punch at Stone's head, and Stone managed to block it, countering with a punch to the jaw. The table was knocked over, Cassandra pressed her back against the wall, hand resting lightly on her gun. She'd thought Stone and the others were dead to the world, but suddenly they'd become lions.

The cowboy in the green shirt tried to knock Stone out with one solid blow, but Stone leaned to the side, slipped it, and hammered him in the pit of his stomach. Green shirt expelled air, and Stone hooked him to the face. The man stood his ground and whacked Stone in the mouth, but Stone threw an uppercut that caught him on the tip of his chin.

Green shirt went stumbling backward, and Stone followed him. Out of the tumult, a man in a fringed buckskin charged

Stone, knife in hand, blade up. Stone reached to his boot and pulled out his Apache knife. The man in the buckskin jacket said, "I'm a-gonna shove that thing up yer ass."

He lunged, and Stone timed him coming in, darted to the side, slashed him from wrist to elbow. The man in buckskin howled in pain, the knife fell from his hand. Footsteps approached from Stone's right, a chair crashed onto his head, he was thrown to the floor. The cowboy stepped over him, looking for someone else to crown. Stone opened his eyes, caught his breath, saw the cowboy with the chair slam Diego, one of the Triangle Spur vaqueros. Stone got to his feet, dived, and brought the cowboy with the chair down.

They hit the floor as fighting raged around them. The entire saloon was brawling, and the bartender screamed: "Stop it, you bastards! You're ruinin' me saloon!"

His voice could barely be heard above the uproar. High on the wall, harem girls watched serenely as angry men busted each other up. Cassandra's fingers tightened around her Colt. If any man made a move, she'd gun him down.

Stone rolled on the floor with the cowboy who'd struck him with the chair. They punched and kicked each other, struggling to gain an advantage, when another cowboy snuck up behind Stone and hit him over the head with the leg of a chair. Stone fell backward, the whites of his eyes showing. The cowboy stood over him, ready to bash him again, when a cuspidor came flying across the saloon. The bilious fluid struck the cowboy in the face, and he was blinded. Gobs of abominable substances rolled down his face, and some got into his mouth. He coughed, vomited, staggered from side to side. Stone rose groggily in time to see a fist streaking toward his nose. He couldn't get out of the way, the fist landed on target, and Stone went stumbling backward into the crowd.

His assailant was named Trevino, and he was wanted for armed robbery in Uvalde County. Trevino followed Stone, trying to kick him in the head. Stone grabbed his leg, twisted, Trevino fell to the floor.

Stone jumped to his feet. A fist streaked out of nowhere and landed on his forehead. He saw stars, wobbled backward. A cowboy jumped on him, dug his teeth into his ear. Stone elbowed him in the guts, slammed him against the wall, hit him with everything he had, and the cowboy dropped like a bushel of eggs.

Somebody got punched through the front window of the saloon, amid shards of glass. The horses at the rail stared through the broken window at their bosses annihilating each other with anything they could lay their hands on.

Somebody fired a shot, and fighting stopped for a second, as men checked whether they'd been struck by a bullet. Then they resumed the struggle. Behind the bar, one cowboy slammed a bottle over the head of a gambler. A freighter whacked a cattle buyer with a full mug of beer. The floor was covered with glass and a variety of liquids, not the least of which was blood. There were groans and screams of pain. Men vomited in corners from punches to the belly. The stench of whiskey was thick in the air, and the harem girls smiled sadly, frozen in time.

Stone got to his feet, staggered, saw a big, brawny bull-whacker headed straight for him, a full cuspidor in his hands. He threw it at Stone, Stone ducked, and it sprayed over the men behind Stone, stinging their skin like corrosive acid, some suffered blurred and distorted vision.

Stone dived on the bullwhacker. They rolled over the floor as other fighting men tripped over them. Somebody kicked Stone in the head as he strangled the bullwhacker, but the bullwhacker's neck was thick and tough as the trunk of a tree. The bullwhacker brought both fists together and bashed them onto Stone's head. Stone saw stars, let go, fell into the endless night.

The bullwhacker raised his fist to punch Stone in the mouth once more, and a table came crashing down onto the bullwhacker's head. It was in the hands of Don Emilio Maldonado, who had gone berserk.

He was the only sober man in the saloon, enraged by Cassandra's rejection. Built like a bull, he punched, kicked, and elbowed his way across the floor, a constant stream of vile Spanish epithets rolling off his tongue.

Stone shook his head and tried to focus on the incredible violence unfolding around him. After so many weeks on the trail, no sleep, insufficient rations, misery, stompedes, crazy injuns, cutthroat rustlers, hailstorms, lightning, water short-ages, working under ramrods who thought more of the cattle, by the time the cowboys hit towns, they were so damned mad they could kill.

A chair flew over him, and men battled everywhere he looked. He got to his feet and turned around. Standing before him was a man with two teeth missing in front and a mad gleam in his eyes as he hurled his fist with astonishing speed toward John Stone's head.

Stone dodged the punch and eased to his left. The man lunged after him, and Stone threw the uppercut. It caught the man coming in and snapped his head back. He was wide open, and Stone shot a jab to his nose. The man raised his hands to protect his face, and Stone hooked him in the left kidney, right kidney, pounded his ear, took him apart. The man stumbled backward, struck the lantern, it fell to the floor.

"Fire!"

Fighting ceased instantly. Stone grabbed Cassandra's hand and pulled her toward the back of the saloon. Slipchuck, wearing a black eye, smashed the rear window with a chair, stood back, and dived out. A tongue of flame climbed the wall. The bartender rushed forward with a bucket of water, threw it, causing a loud hissing and a big smelly cloud of smoke. Cassandra coughed. A shot was fired. Somebody screamed. There was mass confusion, and Don Emilio took hold of her other hand.

"The front door would be better," he said.

"No," replied Stone. "The back door is the best way."

Each pulled Cassandra in an opposite direction. "Let me go!" she shouted.

They dropped her hands. She joined the morass of men trying to get out the back. Stone and Don Emilio followed, but it was difficult to see. Cassandra felt stray hands brush her breasts, her hips, and somebody pinched her behind.

"Son of a bitch!" she yelled.

She grit her teeth, punched, kicked, and an open path appeared before her.

"After you, ma'am," somebody uttered.

She ran through the door into the alley behind the saloon, and the air carried the sweet fragrance of the prairie. She took deep breaths as men poured outside, battered and bruised, coughing, spitting, limping. John Stone, Don Emilio, and Rooney joined her, followed by Slipchuck and the other cowboys from the Triangle Spur.

John Stone was sober and in command. Somehow he'd returned from his stupor, and so had her other men. They laughed, lit cigarettes. The mood changed from savage mayhem to low comedy.

"Jesus—you see the guy what got hit with the spittoon? I thought he was a-gonna die!"

"He *did* die, I think. Last time I seen him, he was a-lyin' on the floor."

What kind of people are they? Cassandra wondered. One minute they tried to kill each other with fists and knives, now they were pals? They examined each other's wounds, roared with glee, enacted great moments from the brawl. They'd tell the story around campfires till the day they died.

Reverend Blasingame approached the back door of the church, looked both ways, inserted the key. A dim light came to him from the parlor, Little Emma held a lantern with one hand, rubbing her sleepy eyes with the other.

Her voice was tiny and soft. "Would you like something, sir?"

"A bit of warm milk and some cookies if you please, my dear. I'll be in my office."

"A man was here to see you. He left a message—it's on your desk."

Reverend Real Estate hung his coat in the hall closet. "What did he look like?"

"Wore a big top hat, sir, and a gold earring." She pinched her fingers around her earlobe. "Think he was from the carnival. Can I see the carnival?"

"You go to the carnival, they'll steal you away from me, put you on display, people will poke their fingers at you."

He climbed the stairs to his office, his face ashen. He opened the door, lit the lamp, sat at the desk. The scrap of paper was in the middle of the blotter, and he hesitated to pick it up. He wiped his mouth with his hand, grit his teeth, and said, "Oh, God, don't do this to me now."

He read the words scrawled in that old familiar style:

Dear Reverend:
Stop by the tent tonight. We got things to hash over.
Jimmy Boy

Reverend Blasingame gaped at the note. What he feared most had come to pass. He closed his eyes and prayed for divine guidance. There was a knock on the door. Emma entered with the tray of cookies and warm milk.

"Did the man say anything to you?" he asked.

"Said he was an old friend of your'n, before you was a preacher."

"Get out of here. I want to think."

He sipped milk and stuffed cookies into his mouth. The only thing to do was consult the Good Book. He picked up his desk Bible and opened it. The pages broke on Jeremiah 40:

> *I will slay Ishmael*
> *and no man will know it . . .*

Carnival tents, bright lights, clowns. Families had come from miles around to see the show, and it attracted an army of drunken, staggering cowboys.

" 'Round and 'round she goes, and where she stops, nobody knows!" shouted a clown wearing a golden earring. "Put your money on the square, my friends, and if your number comes up, you win the jackpot. You can't get a better deal than that. Winners all the time. Put your money down. You, sir!" he said to Stone. "Feel lucky tonight?"

"Not me."

"I feel lucky," Don Emilio said. He walked to the counter and placed his money on a square. Cowboys and farmers covered the other numbers, and the wheel of chance spun against the starry sky. It stopped, a number was called, a whoop went up from the vaqueros. Don Emilio raised both arms in the air. "This is my lucky night!"

They came to the next tent: EGYPTIAN GARDENS.

Another clown stood on a small stage. "Do you like 'em pretty?" he asked. "Do you want 'em to have a lot up here and lot down there." He made comical motions with his hands to indicate portions of the anatomy the cowboys might find appealing. "Well, you come to the right place, my good people! Right here, within this very tent, I have specially trained temple dancers from Cairo, Egypt, and when they shake them hips, you'll want to let it rip. Only a dollar, gentlemen, a mere paltry nothing for the most beautiful dancing girls in the world. Step right up. Don't be shy!"

The crowd moved toward the ticket booth in front of the tent, which emitted eerie music and the rumble of drums. The cowboys and vaqueros got in line, and John Stone was among them. Cassandra held back for a few moments, but curiosity propelled her forward. She felt a grip like steel on her arm.

Don Emilio held her. "That is not a place for *La Señora*."

"I want to see the temple dancers."

"It is disgusting."

"If I weren't here, you'd be first in line."

"That is true, but you are here. Please, señora, let us leave this ugly place. Ride away with me now. I assure you, it will be better than a hootchy-kootchy show."

"I've always wanted to see a hootchy-kootchy show!" She moved toward the door, but he continued to grip her arm. "Let me go!" She pulled herself away from him.

He watched her go. *Women will be the death of me yet.* He moved toward her as the crowd streamed into the tent.

Four musicians played on a rug beside the stage. Lanterns hung from the ridgepole, incense burned in a brazier shaped like the Sphinx.

Cassandra looked for the chairs, but none were provided. The music was exotic and strange, incense tickled her nostrils, and she was the only woman in the crowd.

"Where's the goddamned girls!" somebody hollered.

The flap behind the stage moved, and the clown with a golden earring appeared. "Here they are, direct from Cairo, Egypt, for your pleasure—let's give them a big hand—the Pharaoh's Temple Dancers!"

The drum became louder, and the flute shrieked like an eagle in flight. Three young women dressed in diaphanous garments danced from behind the flap and moved toward the stage, swiveling their hips to the beat of the drum. They had dark skin and exotic features, Cassandra wondered what they were doing here in the middle of a godforsaken foreign land.

They smiled and held their arms outstretched like the wings of birds. They shook their shoulders, and their breasts jiggled beneath the flimsy fabric. A roar went up from the crowd. Cassandra took a step back, because the reaction of the cowboys was as interesting as the dancers themselves.

The men were dazzled by the mere sight of female flesh dancing to music. Cassandra could see lust on their faces. They'd kill at the drop of a hat, but a woman could subdue them with a jiggle.

Her eyes fell on John Stone. A faint smile was on his lips, and she knew what he was thinking. *How can he forget me just because a few women are dancing without clothes?*

Cowboys threw coins onto the stage, and the clown scurried about like a squirrel, picking them up. The band made its strange desert music, and Stone watched the dancer in the middle, her golden skin, the way she shook her hips vigorously. The costume showed her smooth, naked belly, and she wore a ruby in her navel.

"Like her?" Cassandra asked, jealousy in her voice.

"She's all right, but not nearly as lovely as you."

"Maybe you'd like to spend the night with her?"

"Of course not." He returned his eyes to the dancer with the ruby in her navel. She winked at him, or was it his imagination?

Reverend Blasingame moved through the shadows at the rear of the carnival, leaning on his shiny black cane. Two midgets approached, chatting noisily, and he hid behind a tree until they passed.

He could hear the hurdy-gurdy, laughter of children, firing of guns. Carnival night in a small town. It brought back memories.

He waited until the midgets passed, then skirted the rear of the tents. The band played in the Egyptian Gardens, and the barker sold freaks to the crowd. A toothless old lion in a cage growled, his coat half eaten by fleas.

Reverend Blasingame passed the lion and made his way to a tent standing beneath a tree at the edge of the encampment. The sign said MANAGEMENT.

Reverend Blasingame tiptoed toward the tent and peered through a tear in the fabric. A clown with a big red nose, wearing a golden earring, sat at a collapsible table, eating steak and fried potatoes. Papers were stacked around him, and a pile of coins shimmered in the light of the lantern.

Reverend Blasingame looked to his right and left. No one was in the vicinity. He ducked his head and entered the tent.

The clown looked up from his plate of food. He stared at Reverend Blasingame for a few moments.

"I'll be a double son of a bitch," the clown said. "Is it really you, Dickie? I heard you became a preacher. They told me you even got a church."

"The Mount Zion Church of God, on State Street. You should come and pray with us sometime."

The clown laughed heartily. "The greatest flimflam man of them all, dressed as a preacher." He reflected professionally for a few moments, then said, "It's a good costume. Sit down, and let's have a drink."

"Can't drink anymore, I'm afraid, but I'll sit with you."

"Pour one for myself, then." Jimmy picked a bottle and tin cup from a drawer. "Good to see you, Dickie boy. Been a long time. We hit a lot've towns, you and me."

"Many years ago."

"Not that many. Is it ten years? Fifteen? How the time goes, eh, Dickie. Them was the days. We went everywhere together, shared everything including our women. Do you remember the twins from France? Tumblers they were, or was it the trapeze?"

"Tumblers."

"You *do* remember."

"A man doesn't forget things like that, but I have a new life now. You shouldn't've come to the rectory today. I wouldn't want anybody to know about our connection. I lead the religious life now."

"What Bible school you go to? The one that met in the back room of the whorehouse where you and me lived most of the time?" The clown laughed. "God, them was the days, Dickie. We was young and the world was full of good things."

Reverend Blasingame's eyes flashed in the light of the lantern. "God smote me on the forehead, I fell off my horse like Saul of Tarsus. Jesus appeared to me, nailed to the cross. He told me to go forth to all the nations and preach the Gospel."

Jimmy placed his hand on his old friend's shoulder. "Dickie, if I haven't known you so long, I'd make a donation to your church right now. But I remember you when, so save the bullshit for the rubes."

"Christ could perform no miracles in his hometown. They didn't understand how a man can be reborn."

"Folks say you own most of this town, steal from widows and orphans. Don't tell me it's not a good flimflam, because I seen a shitload of 'em, and I knows a good one when I sees it."

"God rewards those who have faith in him. The more you believe, the more you get. But possessions mean nothing to me. Money comes and money goes, but God remains unto eternity."

"You're good. You're damned good. And this flea-bitten carnival of mine is going under. You got a job for me, with your operation, Dickie boy? I could run something for you, like the bank. Somebody told me you own it and lots of other prime businesses in this town. How's about a job for an old friend?"

Reverend Blasingame smiled sadly. "I can't let you live in this town, Jimmy. You might confuse the people. I don't want them to know about my past. No, you must take your carnival and move on." Reverend Blasingame held out his hand. "Let us go in peace and carry forever the memory of two happy young men making their way in the world."

"It won't be that easy, bunkie. You can't toss me away like that."

"I'm not your father, I'm not your mother, I'm not your brother. I'll always remember the happy days we had together, but that was long ago. Don't try to contact me again."

Reverend Blasingame arose from his chair, but Jimmy placed his hand on the pastor's shoulder. "I think you're forgetting something. I saved your ass a few times in the old days, when you didn't have anything. We shared and shared alike. All I'm asking now is a little help."

"You want help, turn to our Savior. He showers his riches on those who revere him."

Reverend Real Estate moved toward the door, and Jimmy grabbed his shoulder again. Reverend Real Estate pushed him away. Jimmy stepped backward, drew a derringer. Reverend Real Estate gazed at Jimmy. "You wouldn't shoot an old friend, would you?"

"I should've left you lying in the alley where I found you," Jimmy said.

"You were so drunk you couldn't walk. You'd fought with the bartender, your nose was broken."

"Still is." Jimmy wiggled his nose. "But I won."

"You always had a good punch."

"Still do."

Reverend Blasingame's eyes were glued to the derringer in Jimmy's hand. "Isn't it sad, when old friends argue?"

"You always did have a short fuse, Dickie. Sometimes I used to think you was crazy."

Reverend Blasingame sat on the chair in front of the desk. Jimmy tucked the derringer into his pocket and returned to his seat. "Sorry I lost my temper," he said.

"A shock to see an old friend again," Reverend Blasingame said. "Ever run into any of the gang?"

"Saw Shorty in Cincinnati last year. Pickin' pockets, burglarizin' houses. Looked like death warmed over."

As Jimmy spoke, Reverend Blasingame lowered his hands beneath the edge of the desk, where Jimmy couldn't see. Silently, keeping his shoulders straight, he withdrew the sword from his cane. When the blade was clear, he said, "It's true, we were brothers, some things never change."

"It's okay to flimflam the rubes, but don't flimflam yourself, Dickie boy. A lot of good men got into trouble that way."

"That lantern is shining in my eyes. Do you think you could move it?"

Jimmy raised his hands toward the lantern. Reverend Blasingame leapt forward and stabbed the sword into Jimmy's back. The scream was muffled with the palm of the pastor's hand, and Reverend Blasingame raised his arm, stabbed Jimmy again.

Jimmy coughed blood, pitched forward, fell to the floor. Reverend Real Estate bent over him, to make sure he was dead. Then he wiped his sword on the tablecloth, slid it into its scabbard. He poked his head outside, heard the hurdy-gurdy, no one in sight. Reverend Real Estate slipped into the darkness and disappeared.

Inside the Freak Show tent, the tattooed man wore abbreviated crimson shorts, flexed arm muscles. Even the bald spot atop his head was covered with images and designs.

He had ships on his cheeks, a dog on his chin, the American flag on his chest, skulls on his shoulders. Interspersed among the larger images was a snowstorm of hearts, diamonds, clubs, and spades. His back was a massive crucifixion at Calvary, with all the principal characters.

He delivered a lecture as the crowd examined him in amazement. "Why do I have so many tattoos? Because I love art, and want to take it with me wherever I go. Even if they throw me in prison, I'll have my art collection. When I go to my grave, my tattoos are the only things I can take with me."

Next attraction: a mustached man inserted a sword into his throat. He left it down there for a while so everybody could see, then pulled it out smoothly, smiled, bowed. Next he placed a torch into his mouth, extinguished it with his tongue. "My kiss of fire."

The fat lady, mountain of rippling pink flesh with a pretty face. She wore a purple garment constructed like a tent, long earrings, several golden necklaces, gold bracelets, a crown sat upon her auburn tresses.

A midget in a funny red suit placed a plate before her. She picked up a fork and dined, her table etiquette impeccable. She was the queen of food.

A drunken cowboy giggled. "You're gonna explode someday, you don't stop eatin'."

"I love food," she replied, munching. "If I don't eat, I get weak. And it tastes so good. Don't you like to eat?"

"Sure, but don't you think you're overdoin' it a little?"

Slipchuck thought her the most beautiful creature he'd ever seen. He yearned to place his weary head upon that exquisite opulent breast. She looked at him and smiled. The others drifted to the next attraction. Slipchuck gazed at her with lovesick eyes. She munched daintily, as if he weren't there.

"Miss," he said. "Could I ask yer name?"

"I'm the fat lady. Can't you see?" She raised her arms, and great globules of fat swung in the air.

He was old, withered, getting arthritis in the knees. She was an ocean of caressing love, just what he needed. He wanted to be a baby again, inside that mass of warm womanly flesh.

"I meant yer real name, miss. I thought maybe we could take a walk later."

"The tattooed man is my husband."

She finished her plate, the midget waiter brought another as the next crowd approached. Wishbone heard the oohs and ahs as new eyes fell on her vast bulk. Somebody laughed nervously. Slipchuck felt sorry for her, forced to exhibit herself for money.

"You come with me," he said. "You won't have to do this no more."

She swallowed her mouthful of food and looked him in the eye. "You couldn't keep me in carrots."

Cassandra approached the strong man. His head was shaved, his musculature gigantic, he wore a black beard, looked like Zeus. His shorts were made from the skin of a Siberian tiger, and he had a single tattoo, a scimitar on his left shoulder. He stood behind the massive iron barbells, huffed and puffed a few times, bent over, snatched the barbell and raised it over his head, his stupendous arms quivering. The audience applauded, and he lowered the barbell to the stage.

"It does not look that heavy to me," Don Emilio said.

"You want to try it?" the strong man replied in a thick Russian accent. "Come. Let us see what you can do."

The vaqueros cheered as Don Emilio stepped onto the stage. He removed his shirt, had a powerful chest and large arms, but not like the strong man's. Don Emilio bent over and placed his hands on the bar. He tightened his fingers, took a deep breath, and pulled. Nothing happened, except his face went beet-red. The barbells hadn't moved an inch off the floor.

"Do not be embarrassed," the strong man said in a deep voice. "There are not many men in this world who could lift this weight."

Don Emilio stepped down from the stage, cursing himself for his pathetic performance.

"Mind if I try?" John Stone asked.

The strong man held out his hand and pulled Stone onto the stage. Stone was drunk, but thought he could lift it. The strong man didn't appear that much larger than he.

He took off his shirt, showing scars and bruises on a solid physique and flat stomach. He rolled his shoulders a few times, then stood behind the bar.

Everyone watched avidly. Cowboys and vaqueros made bets, with the odds two to one against Stone. One of the strong man's bushy eyebrows was raised high. Stone bent down, grabbed the bar, pulled with all his strength.

It rose from the floor, and everyone sucked wind. The sinews of Stone's body quivered as the bar inched higher. His face was wrenched with exertion, and sweat poured out of his forehead. Everybody watched the bar elevate in Stone's big hands, but then his muscles gave out. He grit his teeth and pushed, the barbell fell to the side. He tried to catch it, lost his footing, fell off the stage, landed on the dirt floor. The barbell landed a few inches from his skull.

He shook his head and rose to his knees. The strong man slapped him on the shoulder.

"You are nearly as strong as me," he said. "I am Captain Boris Koussivitsky, formerly of the Don Cossacks, at your service." He bowed slightly from the waist. "I recognize the hat you are wearing."

Stone shook his hand, recognizing another lost soldier. "Let's have a drink."

"I will meet you later in town, if you can call this heap of rubble in the middle of nowhere a town." Koussivitsky curled his upper lip in derision.

They heard a scream outside. "Murder! Bloody murder!"

Everyone dashed toward the exit, Stone's head emerged into the night, a woman waved her hands frantically at the edge of the clearing. They ran toward her, she pulled back the flap of the tent.

They saw a clown with a golden earring and a big red nose lying on the ground, his gaily colored costume covered with blood.

Reverend Blasingame rested against the wall of the vestibule, breathing heavily. The blood-smeared face of his former friend floated before his eyes.

Little Emma shuffled toward him, carrying her lantern. Her eyes widened at the sight of blood on his clothes and hands. Even a smudge on his white clerical collar.

"Make me a bath," he said.

She took a step backward, her distorted features twisted with terror. He wanted to sit, but didn't dare mark his furniture with blood. His cane was covered with blood. *I did it for you, Lord.* He climbed the stairs to his office, took out his vial of laudanum, prepared a drink, returned to the kitchen. Little Emma heated a tub of water on the cook stove.

Reverend Blasingame undressed in front of the fire pit, threw each garment into the roaring flames. He closed the hatch and stood naked beside the stove. Little Emma poured warm water into the circular wooden tub.

"You've killed him, haven't you?" she asked. "He was a friend of your'n. Why'd you do it?"

"Shut up, you little idiot!"

He waited impatiently until she filled the tub, then stepped in, lay down, soaked. The hot steamy water washed his sins away.

5

THE BUCKET OF Blood was even more primitive than the Blue Devil. Its bar consisted of a board stretched across two barrels, and there were no stools or chairs. It was narrow, crowded, lots of whores. Above the bar was a crude painting of young, half-naked ladies in a boudoir.

Stone felt wild and crazy, wanted to punch somebody in the mouth. Cassandra had gone to the Majestic Hotel, and refused to let him stay with her. Don Emilio and the vaqueros had been ordered back to the herd. "Where's that bartender?" He rolled a cigarette, spilling half the tobacco on the floor. The bartender filled his glass, and Stone slugged it down in one shot. The whiskey hit his blood like burning oil. "Do it again!"

"Johnny," said Slipchuck, "you're a-gonna keel over, you keep on a-drinking like this."

"I said do it again!"

Rooney told him, "Every man who drinks is trying to forget something. I know,'cause I'm a drinking man myself. What you trying to forget, Johnny?"

"Everything."

"You're givin' up a good woman," Slipchuck said. "You might be strong with yer arms, but you sure ain't strong here." He tapped his finger against his head.

"Nobody tells me how to live," Stone said thickly. "I do as I goddamn please."

"You'd druther sleep alone than with that fine Texas honey? You're a goddamned fool, ask me. You don't know what's important."

"I don't like this saloon," Stone said. "Been in better pigpens."

He lurched toward the door, bumping into other drinkers, who shunted him to the side. They propelled him outside, and the cool, sweet air struck his nostrils. His head cleared, and he heard the call of a lobo far off on the prairie. *That's where I belong.*

"Where's my horse?"

"Where do you want to go?" asked Rooney.

"I'm going to sleep on the ground like a man."

"Wouldn't you rather have the guest room in my house?"

Stone thought of clean white sheets, a bath, clean clothes. Why did he want to sleep on the ground? What if it rains? They heard a commotion, saw Captain Koussivitsky in the white uniform of the Don Cossacks.

"The carnival is ruined," Koussivitsky said. "I do not have a kopeck, but do I care?" He laughed in his deep baritone voice, and hooked his thumbs in his belt. "Which of you gentlemen will buy me a drink?"

They headed for the nearest saloon, and above the entrance was a sign: McNALLY'S.

One bar on the left, another to the right, tables in the middle, dance floor in back. Above the bar hung the mounted shaggy head of a buffalo, his eyes large and gleaming in the light of the lamps, and he'd been shot full of holes.

They approached the bar. "Drinks all around," Rooney said to the bartender.

He set up the glasses, and all eyes were on Koussivitsky, a giant in his strange Cossack uniform. His left breast was covered with medals, and atop his head sat his black cossack sheepskin hat.

"What're you doing in America?" Stone asked.

"Certain people complained to the czar that my Cossacks raided a village, killed the men, raped the women, ate the babies. I was exiled to Siberia but managed to smuggle myself on a ship at Vladivostok, and next thing I knew, I was in San Francisco. One night I met the clown, here I am. You are strange man. I see in your eyes. You fought in a war. I fought in war too." He raised his glass of whiskey. "To soldiers!" His voice boomed through the saloon.

Most of the patrons had been in the war, they joined the toast. Koussivitsky downed his whiskey in one gulp, as if it were water.

"How I miss vodka," he declared. "Oh, my Mother Russia, when will I see you again?"

Somebody shouted near the swinging doors, a shot was fired. The doors parted, and a horse's head appeared. Men ran out of the way, the horse lurched forward, and a cowboy sat in the saddle, gun in hand. He rode the horse into the saloon, and behind him came another mounted cowboy. Then a third cowboy rode into the saloon, aiming his gun at a lantern. The gun fired, and wood splintered six inches from the flames.

"Hold on!" yelled the bartender. "No horses in this saloon!"

The horses recoiled at the sight of so many men in a small enclosed place. They couldn't move forward due to the close-packed tables. The cowboys hee-hawed, and one fired a shot at the buffalo's head.

The bartenders grabbed double-barreled shotguns from behind the bottles, aimed them at the cowboys.

"Git them goddamn animals outta this saloon!" the lead bartender hollered.

The cowboys looked at two shotguns and saw total destruction. They turned their horses around, and the horses' hooves made a racket against the floorboards. The cowboys rode out of the saloon, and gunshots could be heard in the street outside.

The men in McNally's returned to their whiskey and cards. A fight broke out on the dance floor, and a woman in a dark corner laughed as a cowboy placed his hand up her dress. Stone looked at Slipchuck, and the old ex-stagecoach driver appeared happier than Stone had ever seen him. A happy, foolish grin was affixed to his face, and most of his teeth were missing.

Slipchuck sidled next to Koussivitsky. "You know the fat lady?"

"The woman would eat anything. If there were no food, she would eat the ground. If she sat on you, she would kill you."

"We could build us a little ranch."

"She eat you alive." The captain placed his hand on Slipchuck's shoulder. "Forget her. She is a freak, and only another freak can love her."

At the bar, somebody was punched in the stomach. A glass of whiskey flew through the air and crashed into a wall. Stone remembered the dancing girls at the Egyptian Gardens.

"Who were the Arab women?" he asked Koussivitsky.

"Very sad story," the Cossack said, shaking his great head. "They come to your country to perform in the best theaters and halls, but their American agent cheated them, and they end up with our carnival."

"What'll happen to them?"

Koussivitsky shrugged. "What will happen to any of us? We find another carnival. Or maybe we keep this one. I think there is money, but our employer spent on gambling and bad deals."

A broad-beamed cowboy stood a few feet away, gaping at Koussivitsky. "I never seen such a funny goddamned getup in all my born days."

Koussivitsky narrowed his eyes at him. Everyone stepped out of the way.

"You look like a goddamn ass, you ask me," the cowboy said. "No real man wears silly duds like that. How far you chase the nigger to git that hat?"

"I kill you," Koussivitsky said.

He took a step toward the cowboy, and the cowboy whipped out his Colt. "Hold it right there."

Koussivitsky stopped, his fists balled and his jaw sticking out like the prow of a ship. "Put away that gun, or I break your back."

A shot rang out, the gun flew out of the cowboy's hand. Koussivitsky rushed forward, picked up the cowboy, and threw him against the far wall. The cowboy flew through the air and struck the boards with a terrible crunching sound. Then he fell unconscious to the floor.

Stone returned his gun into its holster. The drinking and card-playing resumed, the piano player struck up a tune.

"You save my life," Koussivitsky said to Stone. "Anything I can do for you?"

"How can I meet the dancer with the ruby in her belly button?"

"That is Seema. I take you to her. She is lonely girl."

They made their way to the carnival at the edge of town. The crescent moon shone over rooftops and chimneys, streets full of drunken men staggering with bottles in their hands or sticking out their back pockets. A cowboy pressed against a whore in an alley, the hem of her dress raised high.

They came to the carnival silent and dark in the moonlight. Koussivitsky entered a tent, leaving Stone with Rooney and Slipchuck. Shouting and gunfire drifted to their ears from the main street of Sundust. Slipchuck rose nervously to his feet.

"Got somethin' to do," Slipchuck muttered.

He walked off nonchalantly, disappeared in the darkness between two tents. Stone rolled a cigarette.

"You don't have money?" Rooney said.

"Haven't been paid yet."

Rooney flipped him a twenty-dollar silver eagle. "Got a feeling you're going to need this."

Stone plucked the coin from the air and pushed it into his pocket. Koussivitsky emerged from the tent, mammoth shoulders and arms, chest like an oversize barrel. "Come, gentlemen."

He led them to the tent, they saw the effulgence of lanterns through the canvas. Inside, the three dancing girls were seated on cushions, attired in brightly colored costumes that revealed much of their bare skin. Incense burned in a bowl, and candles were placed at strategic points on the rug.

Koussivitsky introduced the cowboys to the dancing girls. Seema's eyes were downcast as Stone sat opposite her. The dancing girl named Ishtar served strong coffee in tiny bowls. They drank in awkward silence. Wind ruffled the skirt of the tent, and goose bumps were on the skin of the girls.

Koussivitsky arose, cleared his throat, took Ishtar's hand. They moved toward the darkness at the rear of the tent. Stone looked at Rooney, and Rooney shrugged. He got to his feet and held out his hand to the dancing girl named Ruhla. They left the tent, and Stone was alone with Seema.

"When you were dancing," he said, "did you smile at me?"

She glanced at him shyly and said something in Arabic. She didn't speak English, probably smiled at all the men. He feasted his eyes on her many charms. She was exquisite, trained to entertain royalty, gone bust in Kansas.

She took his hand, he followed her through a network of canvas passageways. She lit a lamp in a small chamber. A rug and blanket lay on the floor, a covered basket sat nearby.

She sat on the rug, and he lowered himself beside her. He wanted to kiss her rose petal lips, but hesitated. Something didn't feel right. What about Cassandra and Marie? He and Seema didn't know each other, couldn't speak, she was a strange frightened creature in a land full of armed men, and he felt like an intruder. She needed the money, and really didn't care about him. Besides, he was supposed to marry Cassandra in a few days. With a sigh of confusion and regret, he reached into his pocket and handed her the twenty-dollar silver eagle.

She stared at it in the center of her palm, and he reeled out of the tiny room. Darkness and tent poles, he pulled his Apache knife, tore a slit in the canvas. Then he stepped through and found himself in another small room. A large dark shape lay on the floor.

"Took the wrong turn," Stone said in an apologetic tone.

Koussivitsky lay on the floor with his massive arms around Ishtar, her slender legs grasping his formidable waist. "Take left turn," the Cossack commander said.

Stone found himself outside. The air was clean, the moon sat on the horizon. He staggered past tents, filling his lungs with the pungent scent of the plains at night. His legs like rubber, he advanced onto open prairie, grass chewed to the roots by herds of cattle that had passed this way. Ahead were hundreds of miles of nothing at all.

He heard an opera of insects and birds. A vast unimaginable land sprawled before him in the light of the moon and stars. His head spun, he lost his footing, reflexes and coordination gone. He landed in a pile of cow manure.

Fatigue hit him like a powerful drug. He closed his eyes and fell asleep instantly, while in the distance the sound of tinkling pianos and laughter in the saloons floated on the cool night air.

A lone horse trudged across the tractless wastes, its eyes half closed. Frank Quarternight slept in his saddle, chin on his chest. His hands rested loosely on the pommel, and he raised up and down with the movement of the horse. Sometimes his eyes opened and he looked around, then fell asleep again.

Nocturnal creatures watched solemnly behind trees and bushes as the gunfighter passed. He dreamed of a bloodied dead girl beckoning to him, dancing voluptuously, luring him onward.

She held out her hand and smiled, and he followed her dutifully across the endless sprawling night.

Slipchuck crawled across the carnival ground like a Sioux warrior homing in on a scalp. He'd searched for the fat lady in every tent, and this was the last one. She had to be inside, sleeping on her bed, resplendent in her nightgown. Maybe if she were alone . . .

He came to the edge of the tent, paused and listened. Nothing was about. He pulled his knife and cut a rope attached to a tent peg. Then he lifted the canvas flap and poked his head inside the tent.

She lay before him, moonlight illuminating her head and shoulders. She wore a white silk nightgown, her belly rose like a continent, her head rested on a fluffy white pillow, her rich thick hair caressed her perfect profile.

Slipchuck crept closer, reached the edge of the bed, brought his beady eyes near her plump hand.

Her fingers were like little fat sausages, and Slipchuck wanted to kiss them. He heard a sound from the other side of the bed. The mattress bounced, and a gun pressed against his forehead.

"Thought I heard a goddamned varmint over here. What you want, you old fart?"

The tattoed man had the drop on him, but Slipchuck had been around the corral a few times. He smiled and raised his hands. "Guess I'm in the wrong tent. Shucks." He tipped his hat. "Sorry to bother you."

Slipchuck gazed at the features of his lady love. Her bosom rose and fell smoothly, and the skin of her face was like the finest Italian marble. He heard the tattoed man shout for help, but Slipchuck's eyes were fixed on the woman of his dreams. He wanted to take off his clothes and crawl into bed with her. Maybe she liked older men. You never could tell about those things.

6

FRANK QUARTERNIGHT SAW the first faint rays of dawn on the horizon. Slouched on his saddle, he steered his horse toward the nearest low prairie hill, dismounted, pulled the saddle off his horse, hobbled it in the midst of plush buffalo grass.

The hump of earth didn't offer much shelter. He unrolled his blanket, noticed the bullet hole in the bottom where the girl tried to kill him, placed his rifle beside him, and lay on the blanket, his Smith & Wesson in his right hand. He rested his head on the saddle and closed his eyes.

The sun rose in the sky. A soft snore escaped his lips. The dead girl danced sinuously before him, her long, slim arms undulating in the dawn light.

Weird and deserted, gaily painted canvas signs hanging limp, the carnival was silent in the morning mist. Its grounds were littered with empty whiskey bottles, chicken bones, cigarette butts. Gone were the crowds, music of the hurdy-gurdy, voice of the huckster. The dancing girls were fast asleep in sheets of fine Egyptian cotton.

A head appeared in the opening of a tent. It was a midget with a shock of red hair, yawning and carrying an axe. He wore only pants, and waddled on short, stumpy legs across the open ground. His head appeared too large for his body, and his arms too short. He came to a stop next to a pile of wood, placed a piece on a stump, raised his axe, chopped.

81

The sound of steel against wood traveled through Sundust. Cassandra opened her eyes. The light of dawn shone through rough muslin curtains. She was accustomed to sleeping on open ground, fully dressed, with boots on in case of stompedes.

Her long blond hair splayed over the pillow, and she wished John Stone were there. Work to do. She threw the covers off and stood beside the bed. Her body was lithe and well muscled as she reached for her britches. She was supposed to meet Collingswood in his office at nine o'clock, and had to hurry. She was selling the herd, her long ordeal was nearly over, or so she thought.

Buckalew finished his last gulp of coffee, then turned the cup upside down and shook the grounds out. He stood, stretched, spat, and walked toward a gunny sack lying near his saddle. He picked it up, it rattled noisily, full of tin cans. He dropped to one knee and laid out cans like a rank of tin soldiers.

He backstepped until he was at dueling distance, wore his gunbelt with the holster on the left side, tied to his leg. His left hand withdrew the gun, it came out smoothly, the leather oiled and slick. He holstered the gun, tensed, held his breath. Then he dropped his left hand, pulled the gun, fired. The sudden detonation sent a flock of birds flying into the air nearby. Dirt kicked a few feet from the cans.

The gun felt awkward and strange in his left hand. He dropped it into its holster, got set, drew again. The stillness of morning was shattered by another shot, and the bullet struck a few inches closer. Buckalew sniffed the acrid gunsmoke and squeezed the gun handle in his fist. His speed was off, so was his aim. But the body was the same, and practice would put everything right.

He was fifteen when he killed his first man. The rich needed bodyguards in a land without police, and he was never strapped for funds again. His daddy said God gave him the talent.

He drew again and fired. The bullet struck closer to the can. He dropped the gun into its holster, got set, yanked again. The sound of the shot pealed across the endless plains.

John Stone opened his eyes. A small furry prairie dog looked at him curiously. The terrible stench of cow manure arose from

Stone's clothing. He climbed unsteadily to his feet, and the prairie dog ran away.

The prairie stretched before Stone, and cattle grazed in the distance. His head ached and he felt sick to his stomach. His mouth tasted foul as a dead rat. He had to get cleaned up.

He spotted a stream, headed for it. Every time his foot came down, a hammer struck his head. *I'm killing myself. I've got to stop drinking.* The night had been full of fights, midgets, the fat lady, a dead clown. He was losing Cassandra, her ranch, children they planned to have.

He came to the edge of the stream, pulled off his boots, unstrapped his guns, emptied his pockets. Then he dived in, clothes, hat, and all. The icy water shocked his mind to attention, he surfaced spouting like a whale. Dirt and manure dropped away, he felt reborn. *I'll never touch another drop of whiskey again in my life.*

Cassandra sat in the dining room of the Majestic Hotel, eating fried eggs, bacon, and grits. The daily routine of beef and beans finally was over.

On the other side of the window, cowboys stirred on benches and in alleys, awakening after their wild night on the town. Wagons and riders filled the street. Storekeepers swept debris from the fronts of their establishments.

"May I join you?" It was Lewton Rooney, hat in hand, wearing a business suit with pants tucked into riding boots. He hung his hat on the hook and lowered himself onto a chair. "Johnny awake yet?"

"I haven't seen him since last night. He was so drunk he could barely stand. He may not make this meeting."

He detected annoyance in her voice. The top two buttons of her shirt were unfastened, her smooth skin was inviting.

"I've seen him drunker," Rooney said.

"Hard to get drunker than he was last night, I'd say." She looked at the clock on the wall. "If he doesn't get here soon, we'll have to leave without him. Slipchuck is still in jail for killing that clown. Do you know a good lawyer?"

"The sheriff doesn't have any real evidence against Slipchuck, from what I've heard. I've got just the man, and he also happens to be mayor. If he can't get Slipchuck off, nobody can."

• • •

Stone walked on the dirt sidewalk, hat low over his eyes. Every time bright light struck his eyes, it was a dagger through his brain. He felt nauseous, and a cigarette hung from the corner of his mouth. His stomach quivered and he felt as though he'd black out at any moment.

He saw a sign: JEWELRY.

Gleaming in the window were bracelets and necklaces encrusted with precious stones. In one corner sat a photo in a silver frame. Stone unbuttoned the pocket of his damp shirt and took out his photograph of Marie. A man in a suit sat behind the counter, reading the *Sundust Clarion*.

"Help you?" he asked, laying the paper down.

Stone held out the picture. "The frame too far gone to fix?"

The jeweler examined it in the bright sunlight streaming through the window. "Might be a few marks here or there, but otherwise should be good as new."

He wrote on a slip of paper. Old clocks and watches hung on the walls, ticking away merrily. The display case contained brooches, rings, stickpins, and in Stone's blurred vision they looked like strange sparkling insects.

"Come back day after tomorrow," the jeweler said, placing Marie on a shelf behind him. "Should have it for you then."

Stone stepped into the street and saw a sign: SHERIFF.

He crossed to the other side of the bustling shopping area. Children played in alleys, jumping over prostrate bodies of sleeping cowboys who stank of whiskey and vomit.

Sheriff Wheatlock looked up from his copy of the newspaper. He was early thirties and wore a mustache.

"Want to see a prisoner name of Slipchuck," Stone said.

The sheriff gazed at Stone thoughtfully for a few moments, then picked a ring of keys from the wall, unlocked the back door. Stone followed him into the jail.

Slipchuck stood with his hands grasping the bars of a cell, broken battered hat on the back of his head, shame on his wrinkled toothless face. He pinched his lips together. "I'd druther face Comanches than jail."

"We'll get you out fast as we can."

Slipchuck held the bars more tightly. "I din't kill no clown, Johnny. You know that, don'tcha?"

"Sure, I know it. But you shouldn't sneak into other people's tents at night. Good way to get shot."

The door opened, and they were joined by Cassandra, Rooney, and an unshaven man in a stovepipe hat. Cassandra said crossly, "Didn't think you'd be up this early, trail boss."

"On time every time," Stone replied from the depths of his severe hangover.

"How're you this morning, you old gopher?" she asked Slipchuck.

"I din't knife nobody," he replied sullenly.

"We've brought you a lawyer. Mayor McGillicuddy, this is Ray Slipchuck, one of my top hands."

Mayor McGillicuddy cleared his throat and stepped forward, fingers gripping his lapels. The fragrance of whiskey accompanied him as he cleared his throat. "What were you doing in the fat lady's tent?"

"I was a-gonna ask her to marry me, yer honor."

"Who was the last person you saw before you were arrested?"

"Them two."

Mayor McGillicuddy looked at Stone and Rooney. "What time did you last see this man?"

"About a half hour before he was caught," Stone said.

"The victim was dead several hours before he was found. I think I can have this man released, but"—he lowered his voice—"I might have to distribute some money to the sheriff."

Cassandra replied, "I own nearly three thousand head of the finest cattle in America—I'm good for it. How soon before he'll be out?"

"An hour."

Slipchuck shuffled nervously in his cell. "Much obliged, boss lady. I can ever do somethin' for you, just ask."

"Stay out of women's bedrooms, if you're not invited."

Cassandra left the sheriff's office, followed by Stone and Rooney. A wagon piled high with buffalo skins rolled past. They came to Dexter Collingswood's office. The clerk admitted them to the inner chamber. Collingswood sat behind his desk. "You didn't tell me you were bringing Mr. Rooney," he said.

"He wants to look at the herd," Cassandra replied.

"I thought you and I were doing business alone."

"You thought wrong."

"But Reverend Blasingame said . . ."

"I don't care what Reverend Blasingame said," she replied. "Mr. Rooney served in the war with my trail boss, and I'm giving him an opportunity to bid for my herd."

"Bid? I didn't realize I was getting into a bidding match!" Rooney chuckled. "Afraid I'll give her a better price?"

"I'll beat anybody's price." He turned to Cassandra. "What're you asking?"

"What I told you yesterday. Twenty-two dollars a head."

The price was high, but Blasingame ordered Collingswood to buy the herd at any price. She wouldn't get the money anyway. "I'll go to twenty-two dollars a head; we can sign the contract right now."

Cassandra wondered what was going on. "Let me get this straight," she said. "We can transact the deal now for twenty-two dollars a head, without you looking at the herd?"

"I don't keep large sums of money in my office. I'll have to go to the bank."

"I bid twenty-three dollars a head," Rooney said.

Collingswood went into a mild state of shock. Twenty-three dollars a head was unheard of in the current market. "Are you crazy!"

"Put up or shut up."

"Your company would never pay such a price!"

"It's my bid. What do you say, Cassandra?"

"I want to get the best price I can . . ."

"Twenty-three-fifty!" Collingswood shouted. He sat behind his desk, face mottled with emotion. People would say he was crazy for paying that much, but orders were orders, and she wouldn't get the money anyway, according to Reverend Blasingame.

"Twenty-four," said Rooney.

Collingswood stared at him in horror. "No herd's worth that amount!"

"My bid stands!"

"But . . ."

"If you don't have a higher bid, we'll consider the matter closed."

"Let me consider your offer," Collingswood said hastily. "Please have a seat. There's whiskey in the cabinet."

Stone made a movement toward the cabinet, but stopped. *When a man wakes up on a pile of cowshit, he's gone too far.*

Collingswood tried to remain calm outwardly, while a wreck inwardly. It was an unprecedented situation in his life. He couldn't agree to more than twenty-four dollars a head, but Reverend Real Estate said make the deal.

"Twenty-four-fifty," he said.

Rooney smiled. "You just bought yourself a herd."

It was a setup, the oldest flimflam in the world, and Collingswood had fallen for it. He wanted to kick himself, but he'd only followed orders. Let Reverend Real Estate worry about it.

"I'll have my clerk draw up the contract," he said. "Take about an hour. You might like to go out for some fresh air and come back?"

Cassandra, Stone, and Rooney left the office, and three doors down was the Pecos Saloon. An old Negro swept the floor, and one sleepy-eyed waitress was on duty. Behind the bar, a man washed glasses in a tub. They sat at a table in back, and the waitress took their order.

"Something fishy's going on," Rooney said. "Collingswood bid prices that are unbelievable. I led him on to see how far he'd go. Wonder what's so special about your herd?"

"They're in first-class condition," Cassandra replied, "but that's not unusual, is it?" She looked at Stone. His healthy tan had become sickly green. He appeared lumbering and stupid. In less than twenty-four hours he'd gone completely down the drain.

"Why would anybody overpay for cattle?" Cassandra asked.

"I've heard rumors about people who've been screwed by the bank, which Blasingame owns," Rooney said.

Cassandra thought of the kindly old clergyman who'd invited her for tea. "I find that hard to believe. He seemed like such a decent man."

"He's never done anything to me," Rooney said, "but the stories keep making the rounds. There's the Sully woman, for instance. Her husband died, the bank took her farm. At first she said Reverend Blasingame cheated her, but then clammed up. It's my guess somebody told her to stop talking about Reverend Blasingame."

"Where is she now?"

"Not far from here, but what makes you think she'll tell the truth? The woman is scared. There's a bunch of local hardcases who more or less do what they want around here. Sometimes people get beat up. Other times they get shot. Their leader is named Tod Buckalew, and he's the fastest gun in town."

Stone and Cassandra looked at each other.

"He and some other men tried to hold us up for a Texas Fever Tariff day before yesterday," Stone said. "Claimed to be a special marshal."

"Sounds like Buckalew and the boys," Rooney replied. "People say they work for Reverend Real Estate, and the dear old pastor is behind most of the shenanigans in this town, but others love him. I'd watch my step if I were you."

Stone said to Cassandra, "Why don't you make the deal with Rooney?"

"If Collingswood'll pay two and a half dollars more a head—do you realize how much that is? We're talking over six thousand dollars in gold. I'm not turning that down. If Collingswood's willing to pay, I'm taking it."

"He'll never pay," Rooney said. "The price is far too much for the market."

"Gunplay?" Stone asked.

"All I can tell you is nobody in Kansas pays that much for mixed longhorns. And he's willing to pay it *sight unseen*. It doesn't add up."

"I'd like to talk with that Sully woman," Cassandra said.

A war whoop erupted from the vicinity of the batwing doors. It was Slipchuck, just released from jail. He pulled up a chair between Rooney and Cassandra. "I knowed I'd find the bunch of yez in a saloon. Where's me whiskey?"

Stone looked at him calmly. "Forget the whiskey, get on your horse, ride back to the herd, and tell Don Emilio to send half his men here immediately, and I want his best guns; we might have trouble."

Reverend Real Estate sat at his desk, eating warm muffins with butter. A napkin was tucked into his clerical collar, and his lips shone with spittle and melted butter. A pen was in his hand, he was writing Sunday's sermon. Little Emma appeared in the doorway. "You called, sir?"

"More butter, and another pot of hot coffee."

Reverend Real Estate felt pleased and even ebullient. The town was growing, his power and wealth increased every day, and Cassandra Whiteside would suck his toes, before he was finished with her. He buttered another roll and stuffed it into his mouth. If a minister wanted to survive in a small community, he had to preach a good sermon. You can't bore them with abstract theological points that nobody cares about. A minister has to put on a good show.

Emma returned with a bowl of fresh butter and a pot of coffee. "Mr. Runge wants to see you."

"Send him in."

Reverend Blasingame slathered another bun with butter, and bit off half. Runge entered the room, his face covered with bruises.

"What happened to you?" Blasingame asked.

"That gang from the Triangle Spur," Runge said sullenly. "Took us by surprise."

"You mean you didn't chase them out of town?"

"Still here."

Reverend Blasingame scowled. "Why didn't you tell me sooner?"

"I came back last night, but the hunch said you was out."

"I was not out. The little darling sometimes becomes confused. Did the Triangle Spur outnumber you?"

"Hard to say. Turned into an all-out saloon war."

"I thought that's what you fellows liked. Maybe you should've had more men. Go to the ranch and round them up. This time don't start anything in a saloon. Wait till they're in the open, and then shoot them up. Take care of this job for me, you'll get a hundred-dollar bonus this month. On your way out, tell Emma I want to see her."

Runge left the office, and Reverend Real Estate finished the rest of his bun. His good mood had been shattered. He'd thought the Triangle Spur cowboys would be run out of town by now.

Emma entered the room. "You want to see me?"

"Come closer, would you, dear?"

Emma approached, a shy smile on her distorted face. She expected a pat on the head for doing something right, but instead he grabbed her ear. "I told you don't let anybody know I was out last night!"

"I didn't . . . I didn't . . ."

"Runge said you did." He slapped her face soundly. "You ever disobey me again, it'll be the streets. And you know what'll happen to you there!" She sniveled and cowered before him as he squeezed her matchstick arms. "I'm letting you off easy this time, but next time you won't be so lucky! Now get out of here and make yourself useful!"

He pushed, and she fell to the rug. He turned toward the plate of muffins. They were cold. "Heat these up and bring them back," he said. "And hurry up. You're not on a vacation."

It was an old unpainted shack near the cattle pens, and the air smelled of manure. A clothesline was stretched between a pole and the shack, and a variety of garments and bedclothes hung upon it. Cassandra knocked on the door.

It was opened by a woman who looked as though she were in her fifties, but probably was thirty-five. Her clothes were soaked and she had a wilted countenance.

"Help you?" she asked, pulling a strand of hair away from her face.

"Mrs. Sully?"

"You got laundry to do?"

Cassandra held out dirty trail clothes. "May we come in?"

"What fer?"

"Want to talk with you."

"Talk here."

"It's about Reverend Blasingame."

Mrs. Sully hesitated, then led them into a small, hot, steamy room. A tub of water, clothes, and suds seethed on the stove, and another tub sat on a table, a washboard sticking out of it. Mrs. Sully stood beside the washboard, where she'd been scrubbing. "What you want to know?"

"I own a herd of cattle, and I'm planning to sell it to a man who works for Reverend Blasingame. You've had dealings with the reverend, and I wanted to know what you think of him."

Mrs. Sully's lips trembled. "Reverend Blasingame is a wonderful man, and if you'll excuse me, I've got work to do."

"I heard he took advantage of you."

"You heard wrong."

Stone looked out the window. "Nobody's around. You can tell us."

Mrs. Sully examined Cassandra's face. "You look like a nice girl," she whispered. "Stay away from Blasingame, 'cause he's a crook. He ruined me, made me do things even the devil would be ashamed of."

Reverend Blasingame chewed his last morsel of muffin and wondered what else to eat. He was still working on his sermon, and later in the day, when the text was in place, he'd practice in front of the mirror.

Little Emma entered the office quietly on tiny pigeon-toed feet, eyes red from crying. "Mr. Collingswood, sir."

"Do we have any pie?"

"Apple pie."

"I'm tired of apples."

"Cake?"

"Yes, and more coffee. Let Mr. Collingswood in."

She backed out of the room. Reverend Blasingame dropped his sermon into a drawer. Collingswood entered the office, his face distorted by excitement.

"What's the matter with you?" Blasingame asked.

Collingswood described his dealings with Cassandra. "That damned Lew Rooney kept jacking up the price, and now we're stuck with twenty-four-fifty a head. We're supposed to sign the contract in an hour, and hand over the gold. We can't pay that much money for mixed longhorns. What the hell you get me into?"

"Hmmm." Reverend Real Estate considered the matter calmly, certain he could solve any problem. He didn't want to back out of the deal, Cassandra Whiteside was a special prize. If Rooney and John Stone were eliminated, she and her herd would be in his back pocket. "When you sign the contract, tell them the bank is out of gold. You'll pay up when the next shipment arrives."

"You're going to close the bank?" Collingswood asked incredulously.

"Telegraph office too. Only for a day or so. We need time until the boys do their job."

"I'm not so sure this is worth the trouble."

"You'll change your mind, once we get Cassandra Whiteside where we want her."

Cassandra returned to Collingswood's office, but the clerk said he wasn't back yet. She sat with Stone and Rooney in the waiting room, beneath a large framed picture of General Grant.

Stone gazed at the picture and reflected on the man who'd won the war for the Union. Grant had been a drunkard and failure before the war, barely able to support his family. At the age of thirty-five he'd sold firewood on street corners, loaded it onto your wagon at no additional cost. Yet that wreckage of a man had gone on to defeat Bobby Lee, the most brilliant fighting general America had ever produced. It seemed a violation of the laws of nature. Were it not for General Grant, John Stone would be living in luxury on the old plantation, Marie would be his wife, he'd have kids, live happily ever after.

Collingswood entered the office, removed his hat. "A hitch has developed, I'm afraid. The bank had so much business the past few days, it's out of gold. A shipment will arrive on the train tomorrow, but we can sign the contract now and get it out of the way. I won't take possession of the herd until the money is paid, of course."

"No point signing the contract, if we haven't got the money," Cassandra replied. "Maybe we should move on to Abilene."

"Abilene's in the same fix we are," Collingswood lied. "Lots of cattle coming through there too. I was you, I'd wait till the money arrived tomorrow."

As soon as Cassandra left his office, Collingswood ran out the back door and sped across town, heading toward the Mount Zion Church of God.

"I need to see the reverend right away," he said, standing in the rectory doorway, "and don't tell me he's busy, because he's never too busy to see me."

Little Emma scurried away, and Collingswood wondered how she breathed through that tangled throat and convoluted chest. He paced back and forth in the parlor, and above the fireplace was a painting of Jesus throwing the moneylenders out of the temple.

Little Emma reappeared out of the darkness. "He'll see you in his office, sir."

Collingswood walked down a dark narrow corridor; he always felt creepy in Blasingame's rectory. The pastor sat at his desk, eating a roast beef sandwich. "Now what?"

"She refused to sign the contract, said she might go to Abilene. I think maybe we should give this one up. Too much trouble."

Reverend Real Estate shook his head slowly. "You don't believe in me."

"It has nothing to do with believing you. We're getting deeper into a mess."

"You must think of the prize. When we get Cassandra Whiteside's herd, your commission will be over five thousand dollars. And let's not forget the party we'll have with Mrs. Whiteside after it's all over. Don't give up now, Collingswood. The fun is soon to begin."

Collingswood left the office, and Reverend Blasingame opened a drawer in his desk, took out his tincture of laudanum. He wondered why Cassandra hadn't signed the contract. Was she getting suspicious?

Reverend Blasingame felt mild trepidation, but recognized it as his own lack of conviction. Maybe a little nap, to renew his strength. He poured himself an extra large drink of laudanum, then lay on the sofa, closed his eyes, thought of Cassandra Whiteside. *The woman needs a good horsewhipping, and I'm just the man to give it to her.*

Cassandra entered the train station. The telegraph operator sat with his feet on his desk, reading the *Sundust Clarion*. The telegraph key before him was silent.

Women came and went in the telegraph station, but not like this. She looked like an Amazon and packed a gun. The telegraph operator arose from his chair. "Ma'am?"

"I'd like to send a message to Abilene."

"Can't do it. Injuns must've cut the wires."

"When'll it be fixed?"

"Tomorrow, I reckon."

Outside, the air was full of cinders from the smokestack of a railroad engine, and it made a horrible racket. Cattle moved onto cars for the last journey of their lives. The air was filled with the stink of excrement and fear.

"I don't know what to do," Cassandra said. "Do you think we should push on to Abilene?"

Stone was about to reply: *Damn right,* but thought of his friend, who'd appreciate the business. "If the train brings gold tomorrow, there's no need to leave Sundust."

"This isn't the first time the telegraph broke," Rooney said. "If Collingswood doesn't buy your herd for the price offered, I'll buy it for market price, so either way it's sold. Why go through the trouble of moving your herd to Abilene?"

Reverend Blasingame lay in fitful sleep upon his sofa, his clerical collar loosened. He dreamed of stabbing his sword into his old friend Jimmy, blood running out of Jimmy's eyes.

He awoke with a start, his stomach ached, he felt the gorge rising in his throat. Jumping up, he pushed his palm against his mouth, then ran in his stocking feet down the hall to the kitchen, gurgling and drooling. It felt as though he were going to die.

He charged into the kitchen, saw Emma mopping the floor, and the mop was nearly twice as tall as she. She stepped back in terror as Reverend Real Estate dropped to his knees in front of the mop bucket, bent his head, and retched semidigested buns, butter, and coffee into the dirty water.

He thought his stomach, intestines, and spleen would come up too. His squat, chubby body was racked by paroxysms of regurgitation, tears rolled from his eyes, his innards felt broken loose from their moorings.

He grasped the pail frantically, it slid on the floor. His knees were soaking wet, as was his shirt. He glanced to the side and saw Little Emma covering her deformed mouth with her hand, laughing at him.

"You little bitch!" he shouted, lunging for her, but the floor was slippery and he lost his footing. He fell onto the mop bucket, and it tipped over. A wave of filthy water rolled across the kitchen floor, and Reverend Real Estate lay belly down in the middle of it, gritting his teeth. The language of the gutter spewed from the mouth of Sundust's beloved pastor.

• • •

John Stone stood with a towel wrapped around his waist, shaving his beard. He'd just taken a bath, the tub of dirty water next to the kitchen stove. His true face came into view beneath the thick beard he'd worn since San Antone.

The door opened, and Cassandra entered. "I bought the biggest size they had," she said, dropping new men's range clothing onto the table.

He scraped away his last remnant of beard, washed his face in the basin, dried it with a towel. "How do I look?"

She was surprised by his appearance, because she'd never seen him clean-shaven before. He was quite handsome in a scarred, rugged, beat-up way.

He donned new black pants, a green and blue checked shirt, black socks, then sat on a chair and pulled on his boots. She watched from the window, sun aureoling around her golden hair. Gone was the filthy drunkard of last night. This man could turn a lady's head. He stood, strapped on his gunbelts, and tied the holsters to his legs. "Feel like a new man," he said.

He walked toward her, a strange gleam in his eyes.

"What are you going to do?" she asked.

He kissed her, she was taken by surprise, arms flailing helplessly, off balance. He smelled like soap, carried her up the stairs two at a time. "I've always wanted to get you on a bed," he said.

She wanted to tell him they shouldn't, because they were having so many problems, but she'd wanted him on a bed too. He lowered her to the sheet, unbuttoned her shirt, his lips touched her throat. The feather mattress was soft and bouncy as he rolled on top of her. She decided the problems could wait till later.

Buckalew looked at the row of cans in front of him. The neckband on his hat was soaked with perspiration, his right hand stung, his left was poised over the holster.

He imagined John Stone standing in his floppy leather leggins, tall son of a bitch. It was showdown in Sundust, both in the middle of the street, everyone watching, especially the women. Probably be night, lanterns shining in the saloons.

His hand flicked to his gun. It was clear of his holster in a split second. The shot fired, its sound echoed across the grassy

wastes. A smile broke out on Buckalew's face as the can flew
into the air and kissed the sun.

Don Emilio wore a scowl, and his vaqueros were afraid to talk
as they drank coffee beside the chuck wagon. Don Emilio had
been thinking about Cassandra ever since leaving Sundust.

She was there with John Stone, his arch rival, instead of
with him. Don Emilio tried hard to make her love him, but
every effort failed. He'd almost won her last night, but the
hootchy-kootchy show got in the way. Only a woman with a
sick mind would see such an outrageous spectacle.

*What kind of women go to saloons? What kind of man
permits his woman to do such things?*

"Somebody is coming, Don Emilio!"

Don Emilio saw a rider heading toward them at a full gallop.
A small man crouched low in the saddle, bearded face nearly
resting on his horse's mane, crazy old Slipchuck.

The vaqueros and cowboys gathered around. They knew
trouble came on hard-ridden horses. Slipchuck pulled back his
reins, and his horse dug in his hooves. The horse's floppy lips
frothed, and the animal shuddered as Slipchuck jumped down
from the saddle.

Slipchuck took off his hat, wiped his forehead with the back
of his arm. "Need some he'p in town!" he said. "Might be
gunplay."

John Stone and Cassandra lay in the afterglow of love, arms
around each other, cheeks touching.

"You and I want the same things," Stone whispered. "Marriage, a home, beautiful strong children who'll build on what
we leave behind. Maybe there's somebody better than me,
but you might die before you find him." He kissed the tip
of her nose.

Cassandra felt torn between the John Stone who was a
drunkard, and the one in bed. She whispered into his throat,
sending thrills up his spine: "I don't want to marry a man
who loves drink more than me. If you could stop drinking,
I'd marry you."

"You can't expect a man to suddenly *stop* drinking. I've just
hit town after two months on the trail. A man needs a drink.
You don't want a dried-up old teetotaler, do you?"

"I wouldn't mind you having one or two drinks every now and then. Maybe even three or four, but that's enough. You drink until you can't move."

"Let's cut a deal," Stone said. "Three or four drinks every now and then, but no more. How about it?"

They heard footsteps on the stairs. Cassandra moved away from Stone and pulled the covers to her chin. There was a knock on the door.

"Come in," Stone said.

Rooney entered the room, attired in suit and tie, carrying a bottle of whiskey and three glasses. "I hope you've found the accommodations to your liking?"

Cassandra turned red with embarrassment, while Stone was relaxed and jovial. Rooney filled a glass with whiskey, passed it to Stone.

"Just finished transacting business with Mr. Bennington," Rooney said, "but can't pay him off. No money and no telegraph. The mayor's holding a meeting to decide what to do. Sundust's cut off from the rest of the world, and not a damn thing we can do about it."

The buzzard rode great thermal updrafts high in the sky, his gigantic wings outstretched, head jerking about as he examined the land for food.

Some days he soared vast distances without finding anything. Other days there'd be dead creatures everywhere, and he gorged his belly. One eye looked down at the earth, the other searched for comrades diving toward the ground, the signal they'd found something. He searched every inch of prairie methodically, his sharp eyes told him the difference between rock, shadow, dead creature.

He saw movement far on the horizon, dropped lower, stuck his red head and gold beak forward for a better look. It was a horse, and near it a body. The buzzard's mouth watered as he dived. He inclined his left wing and made a long swooping circle through the sky. His eyes were fixed on the form on the ground, watching for movement.

Frank Quarternight lay with his head beneath the blanket. It was warm, he slept fitfully. There was a strange sour sensation in his body, as if his blood turned to acid. Sometimes he wasn't sure whether he was awake or asleep, as he dreamed of the girl dancing weirdly around him, waving her arms and making odd gestures with her hands.

She danced closer, dropped to her knees, bent low, kissed his face. He opened his eyes, saw blond hair and a skull grinning at him. With a blood-curdling shriek he hurled the blanket off him and fired.

The shot reverberated across the plains, and his horse looked at him curiously. The girl vanished into thin air, another bad dream. With a growl, he pushed his gun back into its holster. The tepid water in his canteen tasted of alkaline. He looked toward the sky, saw a buzzard flying away.

He covered his head with the blanket. It smelled old and woolly, but he couldn't sleep with the sun in his eyes. He felt a dull, thudding ache in the middle of his brain. There was a time when he could fall asleep anywhere, but it wasn't so easy anymore.

His chest rose and fell evenly, and the girl crept from behind a bush. She stood before him and removed her bloodied dress, stockings, shoes. Naked, she shook her hips lewdly, resuming her strange serpentine dance, breast covered with fresh wet blood.

7

IT WAS LATE afternoon in Sundust. Mayor McGillicuddy stood on the veranda of the Drovers Cottage. "We've had enough!" he shouted, waving his fist in the air. "It's time to take action!"

A roar went up from the crowd of merchants, ranchers, cowboys, and farmers assembled in the street.

"They can't do this to us!" the mayor hollered. "We're sovereign citizens and demand the same rights as other citizens! As George Washington, the father of this great nation, once said . . ."

"Arrest 'em!" somebody shouted.

"That's right!" another man yelled. "Throw 'em in the hoosecow!"

Mayor McGillicuddy held up his hand. "You can't arrest somebody without a writ of habeas corpus!"

"Shove it up yer ass!"

Men in the crowd grumbled and brandished guns as they moved down the street toward the bank. The mayor ran in front of them. They pushed him out of the way. He nearly fell to the ground, his hat fell off. "We're law-abiding citizens!" he sputtered into his mustache. "We can't take the law into our own hands!"

They came to the bank. Two cowboys went inside while the crowd seethed in the street.

"String the son of a bitch up!"

The assembly grew. Somebody fired a shot. The door to the bank opened, and its president, Marcus Strickland, appeared.

99

Everybody booed as he hooked his thumbs into his red suspenders and puffed out his chest. He was portly, in his sixties, with a gold chain hanging over his purple brocade vest.

"What seems to be the problem here!"

"We want our money!"

"Don't have any at the present time!" Strickland replied. "Another shipment arrives tomorrow on the train, please let's be patient!"

Somebody fired a shot, and the bank window cracked like a spiderweb. Strickland ran into the bank and slammed the door. The crowd surged forward, but Mayor McGillicuddy stood in front of them.

"Citizens—you don't know what you're doing!"

They rushed the door, aimed their guns at the lock.

"Hold it right there!" yelled Sheriff Wheatlock. "Next man touches that building, he's a dead son of a bitch!"

A double-barreled shotgun was pointed at them. The crowd pulled back. Sheriff Wheatlock stood beside Mayor McGillicuddy. "We live by the law in this town!" the sheriff bellowed. "Any man wants to rob this bank has to git by me!"

No one moved. A double-barreled shotgun was too powerful an argument to ignore.

"Crowd's too big!" the sheriff said. "Break it up!"

"What 'bout our money?"

"Don't know nothin' 'bout money. We got an ordinance against crowds in Sundust, so git yer damned asses movin' on out of here!"

Men grumbled angrily while Sheriff Wheatlock stood firmly at the door. You can bust up a saloon or shoot a man in the street, but don't ever mess with the bank.

Reverend Blasingame sat at his desk, still working on his Sunday sermon. The finale was the most important part, because immediately thereafter the ushers passed the collection baskets around.

The best kind of sermon made them feel guilty, and at the end you offered salvation. They could buy their way into heaven, and he'd build a great temple on the plains, draw pilgrims from all over the world.

Little Emma curtsied jerkily. "The man from the bank here to see you."

The most crucial part of the sermon was being interrupted. Could he ever capture this special moment again? Marcus Strickland walked into the office, hat in hand, and beside him was Sheriff Wheatlock. Reverend Blasingame spun around in his chair and said angrily, "I thought I told you two never to come here!"

"Emergency," Strickland said. "The people are ready to tear the town apart. I think we're headed for big trouble. Why did you close the bank?"

"I have my reasons. Keep it closed." Reverend Real Estate looked at Sheriff Wheatlock. "I sent for the boys. They'll keep law and order. This'll only last another day. Then the whole incident will be forgotten."

"You weren't there," Strickland said. "They weren't trying to break down your door."

"Shut up." Reverend Blasingame looked at the sheriff. "Don't be afraid to shoot. Sometimes people need an example."

"They was talkin' about appointin' a new sheriff."

"Don't give up that badge to any mob. You'll be the laughingstock of Kansas if you do."

"What if they ask the Army for help."

"Don't worry about the Army. Tomorrow the bank'll be open, and this'll be memory."

Strickland said, "Why can't we open the bank now? We can avoid this trouble."

"I'm sure there are a million other jobs you can get."

Strickland noted the irony. It was difficult to find good jobs in banking if you'd been arrested for embezzlement in Vermont.

Strickland and Wheatlock left the office. Reverend Blasingame returned to his sermon, but his mood had soured. He wasn't ready to give up Cassandra Whiteside. Her herd represented a great deal of money. He could enlarge the church, hire more gunfighters. Building an empire was a step-by-step process, and he was still on the rudimentary levels. It wasn't every day that a rich, beautiful, defenseless widow came along.

He was an old man, getting weaker every day, feeling deep cravings for young women. Absentmindedly he pulled the cord above his head. The face of a proud woman in subjugation, medicine for his soul.

Little Emma stood in the doorway.

"Do we have cake?"

"Don't eat more cake, sir. Remember what happened this morning."

"How dare you say such a thing to me! Bring me a piece of cake and another pot of coffee, you little imp!"

She fled the room, and he lowered his hand, returned to his sermon. The boys were expected any moment, and his plan would move to fruition. Eve would be brought down, and all the angels in heaven would rejoice.

"Send a delegation to the governor!"

The crowd was gathered in the First Baptist Church of Sundust, a small ramshackle structure not far from the stockyards. The walls were in need of paint, half the pews were broken. Reverend Donald Tipps sat beside the altar, sad eyes, black suit threadbare at the knees and elbows, ex-Army chaplain for the Union during the Rebellion.

Voices in the crowd shouted back and forth. Everyone had a different opinion. "I say we remove the sheriff from office!"

Koussivitsky entered the church, wearing a cowboy outfit. He spotted Stone standing against the back wall.

"What is going on here?" Koussivitsky asked. "Bank is closed? I have no money anyway. What the hell do I care? Who is going to buy me a drink?"

On the podium, the mayor spoke of civic responsibility. Koussivitsky wrinkled his nose as if he'd smelled something distasteful. "These people, I know what they are like. They would shiver in boots if anybody said *boo* to them. They are not fighters. If I had one squad of Cossacks, I could destroy this town and five more like it." A wistful look came to his eyes.

"I say send a delegation to the governor, request him to investigate the goings-on in this town!"

Koussivitsky cast a jaundiced eye upon the farmer who made that statement. "They are not going to do anything," he said derisively. He made a fist, and it was big as a cabbage. "The only thing people respect is *this*!"

Stone turned to Cassandra. "By the way, I've hired this gentleman."

Koussivitsky wore the biggest hat she'd ever seen, and his bulging muscles strained the seams of his clothing. Strapped to his leg was a Remington, and it looked like the same model

Truscott used to carry. If only Truscott were here.

"There may be shooting," she said to him.

He shrugged his enormous shoulders. "What is a little shooting?"

"The new man gets the worst jobs. I'm telling you now so I won't hear any bellyaching later."

Koussivitsky placed both hands on his stomach. "My belly never ache unless I eat too much piroshki."

They walked toward the Majestic Hotel. The atmosphere of the town had undergone a change. Most nonsaloon establishments had closed. The train wasn't chugging at the station. The town was dying.

"Maybe we should leave for Abilene," Cassandra said.

"Can't go now," Stone replied. "Half the men from the herd are on their way here."

What would Truscott do? She tried to conjure him up in her mind. He'd go to great lengths to help an old friend, which is what Rooney was to John Stone.

They passed through an alley and disappeared from view. A few moments later twenty riders appeared on Main Street, headed by Runge. They stopped in front of the Blue Devil Saloon and hitched their horses to the rails.

Mr. Peabody watched from the jewelry store across the street, wondering whether to close for the rest of the day. Trouble was brewing, and he didn't want any part of it.

The door to the shop opened, and a fashionably dressed woman entered. Mr. Peabody had never seen her before. She placed a broken bracelet on the counter. "Can you fix this?"

He picked in up, and it was gold studded with emeralds and rubies. "How long will you be in town?"

"Till the train comes tomorrow. May I see that picture over there, please?"

She pointed to the bent silver daguerreotype of Marie, and he handed it to her.

"Who left this?" she asked.

"Cowboy."

She handed the picture back. "He has my sympathy."

"You know her?"

"Sorry to say I do."

"The cowboy was looking for her. Do you know where she is?"

"Fort Hays."

Mr. Peabody wrote the information on a sheet of paper. "What's your name, ma'am?"

"My husband is Major Salter, and we're staying at the Majestic Hotel. We've heard you're expecting a minor war today. What do you think?"

"Could heat up," Mr. Peabody admitted. "Might be a good idea for you and the major to stay in your room, till the train comes."

Reverend Blasingame entered his church, carrying his black leather Bible under his arm. Scattered in pews before him were men and women praying. He walked to a toothless old man, who looked up with pleading eyes. "My gran'daughter died this mornin', Reverend. Had the croup, and she was only nine month old. Why did God take her away?"

"Perhaps the answer can be found in Job fourteen:one: 'Man that is born of a woman is of few days, and full of trouble. He cometh forth like a flower, and is cut down: he fleeth also as a shadow, and continueth not.' "

Reverend Blasingame moved toward a bony woman wearing a homespun dress, sobbing into her hands. "My husband's took to drink. We don't never see him no more. Farm's fallin' apart."

He handed her a twenty-dollar gold piece. "Remember Luke twelve:fifteen: 'A man's life consisteth not in the abundance of the things which he possesseth.' And Luke twelve:thirty-one: 'But rather seek ye the kingdom of God; and all these things shall be added unto you.' Also Proverbs eight:nineteen: 'My fruit is better than gold, yea, than fine gold; and my revenue than choice silver.' "

He moved to a young woman sitting in another pew. "The peace of God be with you." he said.

Her face was distraught. "We're decent God-fearin' people, we work hard all day, but things git worser and worser. Why is it good people suffer, while the bad git rich?"

"The Bible answers all our questions, sister. There's Ecclesiastes nine:eleven: 'The race is not to the swift, nor the battle to the strong . . . ' "

Reverend Blasingame squinted into a dark corner. It was Runge beckoning to him. The pastor walked toward him. "I told you never to come here! Go to the rectory, you idiot!"

Runge was crestfallen. Hooking his thumbs in his gunbelt, he moved toward the front door of the church.

Reverend Blasingame cursed inwardly. They were all so stupid. He came to his parlor, where Little Emma dusted furniture.

"Have you made pie today?" he asked.

"In the oven, sir."

"Bring me a slice as soon as it's out, with a dollop of whipped cream on top."

He entered his office, and Runge was already there, seated glumly on a chair in front of the desk. Reverend Blasingame placed his hand on Runge's shoulder. "I'm not angry at you, my boy. Just remember you mustn't ever speak with me in public again, clear?"

"Things is heatin' up out there, whether you know it or not. There's an armed crowd in front of the Majestic Hotel, and I think we'll have to shoot a few of 'em."

"I'll leave that to your discretion, but first I want you to gun down two men: John Stone and Lewton Rooney. I don't know where they are—you'll have to ask Collingswood. Then run the other cowboys from the Triangle Spur out of town, but don't harm the woman, and don't let her get away."

"There's an Army man in town. Might stick his big nose in."

"Shoot him too, he gets in your way."

Cowboys and Mexican vaqueros rode down the main street of Sundust, grimy and ragged, wearing extra belts of ammunition crisscrossed over their chests, wilder than coyotes. Alderman Shaeffer watched them from behind a window in the Majestic Hotel. In another corner of the lobby, Mayor McGillicuddy conferred with civic leaders. They still hadn't settled on a plan of action.

"More armed men just showed up," Shaeffer said. "I think we ought to send somebody to Reverend Blasingame himself and talk this thing out."

"Why Reverend Blasingame?" Mr. Hudspeth asked. "Don't tell me you believe them lies about him ownin' this whole town? I don't know about you, but I think he's the most maligned man in Sundust. You spent more time in his church, you'd know that yourself."

"He sure knows his Scripture," somebody said.

The cowboys and vaqueros from the Triangle Spur came to a stop in front of the Blue Devil Saloon. They climbed down from their horses and threw their reins over the hitching rail. Don Emilio pushed back his sombrero and looked down the street. He could feel the crazy energy of men ready to kill each other.

"We must find *La Señora*," he said. "Search every place of business, and hurry. I do not like the looks of this place."

Small and spiderlike, Runge entered Collingswood's office. He moved toward the desk, his eyes darting about nervously, his face flushed with hidden emotions. "The reverend said you knew where this Whiteside woman and her cowboys are."

"Lew Rooney's house, last thing I heard."

Runge headed for the door.

"What're you going to do?" Collingswood asked.

"Kill 'em."

Collingswood blinked. "Did you say you're going to *kill* them?"

Runge spun around and faced him. " 'At's right."

"You invade a private home and shoot people, there'll be serious trouble. This town's a powder keg, and it won't take much to set it off."

Runge snorted derisively. "Nobody'll do nothin' in this town."

"There's an Army officer here. We'll be under martial law."

"Reverend said shoot him too." Runge stepped back toward the desk. "The trouble with you is you're a coward!"

"Now just a minute!"

Runge flicked his hand, and suddenly his gun was out. "You goddamned yellowbelly."

Collingswood stared at the gun. Realization of his fragile mortality came over him.

"I ought to kill you," Runge said. "You'd be the first to stab the reverend in the back."

Collingswood saw the lunatic sheen in the young man's eyes. "I may not be much of a believer," he admitted, his eyes on the barrel of the gun, "but I try."

"Try harder. Don't go shootin' your mouth off to the wrong people."

Collingswood stood trembling behind his desk after Runge left. Never in his life had anybody pointed a gun at him. His heart beat rapidly. He wanted to get out of town, but the plains were full of injuns and men who killed for fun, like Runge.

He put on his stovepipe hat and ran out of his office. The street was full of armed men, their mood a palpable malignant force. He'd been earning good money, everything had been fine, and now the world was exploding.

He came to the back door of the rectory and didn't even bother to knock. He entered the vestibule and headed for the stairs. Little Emma came running out of the shadows. "You can't—you can't!"

He pushed her out of the way and vaulted up the stairs three at a time. Moving swiftly down the hall, he came to the door of Reverend Blasingame's office. He threw it open and saw Reverend Blasingame posing in front of a full-length mirror. Reverend Blasingame turned to him suddenly, and Collingswood saw an expression of animal terror on the pastor's face. There was silence for a few moments, and Collingswood was surprised to see the mirror. Usually it was covered with drapes, and he'd assumed it covered a window.

"What're you doing here?" Reverend Blasingame asked. "How dare you barge into my office this way!" He pulled the cord and closed the drapes.

"Had to speak with you," Collingswood said breathlessly. "Runge just tried to kill me."

"Too bad he didn't go through with it."

Collingswood was stung by the remark. "But . . . but . . ."

"You're falling apart, Collingswood. I suggest you go to church and pray for God's protection."

"I don't think you understand what's going on. The street is full of angry drunk cowboys with guns who want to get paid. You can't expect civilized behavior from them. Runge just told me he's going to kill people. You don't understand: once the shooting starts, there'll be a bloodbath."

"Ever think that might be what this town needs?" Reverend Blasingame asked. "We'll get new people who don't know about certain relationships that have existed since the beginning."

Collingswood stared at Reverend Blasingame as if seeing him for the first time. "You're talking premeditated massacre."

" 'A cleansing process' would be my choice of words."

"*You* might be killed too, once it starts. A lot of people know about you, and this might be the first place they come."

"Runge and the boys'll take care of me. Shopkeepers and cowboys won't dare stand up to them."

Collingswood wanted to go somewhere quiet and think. It was turning into the worst nightmare of his life. Reverend Blasingame reached for his cane. The man knew too much, and who knew what he'd say. But he was necessary to broker the deal with Cassandra Whiteside.

Reverend Blasingame leaned his cane against the wall. "You talk to the wrong person, you'll be shot."

"I would never betray you," Collingswood said, a tremolo in his voice.

"You're distraught. We all say things we don't mean. Go home and lie down. Have a cup of coffee."

Collingswood departed, and Reverend Blasingame sat behind his desk, finger against his chin. Collingswood was coming apart at the seams. Maybe it was time to replace him with a more stable cattle broker, one who wouldn't shrink at the sight of a little blood.

"Any food in this house?" Cassandra asked.

"I eat in saloons," Rooney said. "We'll have to go out."

Stone looked at the backs of buildings that faced the main street of Sundust. A crowd of men erupted out of an alley. Stone drew his Colt, Koussivitsky dropped to one knee before the other window. The fading sunlight fell on Don Emilio Maldonado, who carried the ranch's double-barreled shotgun. Following him were cowboys and vaqueros from the Triangle Spur.

"Our worries are over," Stone said. "We can go anywhere we want now."

Don Emilio and his men crowded into the room, and they looked like a hive of angry bees. Manolo, a short, stout vaquero, saw the bottle of whiskey on the table. He pulled out the cork with his teeth, leaned back, and guzzled it down like water.

"What is the problem?" Don Emilio asked. His eyes fell on John Stone. "A miracle—the *borrachín* is sober. The Madonna herself must have appeared to him. But it will not last long. A *borrachín* cannot stay away from his whiskey. He will be crawling on the floor soon, you will see."

Stone glowered at Don Emilio. "I'm getting sick of your insults."

The Mexican moved his hand toward his gun. "Do what you have to, amigo."

"I'm still hungry," Cassandra said.

"The restaurant in the Majestic Hotel is probably your best bet," Rooney told her. "It's as safe as you can get in this town, and besides, you have your own army with you."

The knife fighters, saloon brawlers, sharpshooters, and ex-soldiers surrounded Cassandra. "Let's tie on the feedbag, boys," she said, and hitched her thumbs in her gunbelt, sauntering like Duke Truscott toward the door.

"I'm not sure this is a correct course of action for us to follow," said Mayor McGillicuddy, walking down a corridor on the third floor of the Drovers Cottage.

He was followed by Dennis Shaeffer, owner of the dry goods store. "You'll have to talk with him. Irresponsible not to. He represents the federal government."

They came to the door, Mayor McGillicuddy knocked. There was no answer. He knocked again. "Perhaps they're out."

"Desk clerk said they're in."

The mayor knocked again, heard footsteps. The door was opened by a man with a black mustache, attired in a robe, a grouchy expression on his face. "What you want!"

"I'm the mayor of Sundust," McGillicuddy said, trying to smile, "and I'm afraid we're having a little problem. Since you're Army, we thought we should consult with you. We're expecting serious gunplay. I mean large numbers of men. A town-sized war is what I'm talking about here."

A woman appeared to the right of her husband, and she too wore a robe. They'd been in bed in the late afternoon, Mayor McGillicuddy realized.

"I told you before," she said to her husband. "Every man's walking around with a gun, talking about shooting some-body."

"Nothing I can do about it," Major Salter said. "I'm not here on official duty."

"I'm asking for you help, Major, and Mr. Shaeffer here, our chief alderman, is my witness."

Many rising military careers had gone aground on civilians, and Major Salter didn't want to take the chance. He wore a looping four-inch scar on his right cheek, and wanted a brigadier's star. "What d'you want me to do?"

"Maintain law and order, with the armed citizens of town."

"Who're they fighting?"

"About twenty gunmen, and don't ask who they're working for. We've got our suspicions, but can't prove anything."

Major Salter stood straighter, a military man could be seen beneath the light cotton civilian robe. "Tell every man in this town to bring his weapons, ammunition, and family to this hotel. We'll fight them from here."

Cassandra and her men reached the main street of Sundust, saw the angry armed crowd. Children ran among the adults, aiming their forefingers like the barrels of guns. A bottle came flying through the air, sailed past Cassandra's head, shattered against the wall of a building.

"It's got worse," Rooney said. "Maybe you should go to Abilene after all, and I'll come too, until things settle down here. To hell with my commission."

"I think he's right," Stone said. "Let's go to the stables."

Something big and wide crashed into him, knocking him back a few feet. A cowboy two inches taller than he, with walrus mustaches, stood in front of him.

"Watch where the hell you're going!" the walrus said thickly, and whiskey fumes spewed from his lips.

Stone moved away, but the cowboy lurched into his path.

"Wait a minute," the cowboy said. "I ain't finished with you."

"I'm finished with you," Stone said. "You don't get out of my way, I'll go right through you."

Stone saw the punch coming for a long time, the cowboy's reflexes were so slow. It was easy to lean to the side, and the punch whistled past Stone's ear. Before the cowboy's arm was fully extended, Stone was inside. He pounded the cowboy's left kidney, right kidney, then threw one over the top.

His fist connected with the side of the cowboy's head, and the cowboy wobbled. Stone slammed him in the face, and he went flying into the arms of his friends.

Stone pulled the gloves more tightly on his hands as he moved toward Cassandra and the others. "Let's get out of here," he said. "I've got a feeling this is only the beginning."

Reverend Blasingame studied long columns of ledgers as Abigail Thornton entered his office, wearing a black dress. She pointed toward the window. "Do you know what's going on down there? Have you any idea what you're doing?"

"You appear overheated, my dear. Sit, I'll have Emma bring you some warm milk."

"Need something stronger than warm milk. You don't open that bank, you'll have the cavalry here. I've heard people say you should be lynched."

Reverend Blasingame smiled. "We lynch rustlers, horse thieves, and niggers, but preachers generally die from natural causes."

She pointed her long bony finger toward him. "The crowd is getting ugly. This town could be burned to the ground."

"Nonsense."

The door opened, and Runge entered the room. He poised his mouth to talk, but the syllable caught in his throat when he saw the schoolmarm.

"You can speak freely in front of her," Blasingame said.

Runge was small and wiry, backlit from the lantern in the hall. "The crew from the Triangle Spur's pullin' out of town, with the woman. Should we go after 'em?"

Reverend Blasingame thought for a few moments, then a smile grew on his face. "Bushwhack them, but bring back the woman alive."

A grin appeared on Runge's face. "What you want the woman fer, Reverend?"

"There's one more thing I want you to do. Shut Collingswood's mouth permanently."

Runge left the office, and Reverend Blasingame turned to the schoolmarm. An expression of terror was on her face.

"What's wrong, dear?" he asked, moving toward her.

"Don't touch me," she said, taking a step back. Her eyes were wide, the blood had drained from her face.

His eyes crinkled with kindness. "You've heard things that perhaps you shouldn't've. I told you never to come here."

She was speechless, mouth hanging wide, hair frizzled. She moved toward the door, but he got in her way, raising his arms. "What's your hurry? You don't need to leave so soon. We have so much to talk about." He moved closer to her, and her back was to the wall, fingernails digging into the wallpaper. "I know what's wrong," he told her. "You don't understand your Scripture. Christ himself said he brings not peace, but a sword."

"I won't say anything," she replied in a quavering voice. "You can trust me."

He reached up suddenly and grabbed her throat. His thumbs clamped down hard, and she gagged as she reared back her fist. He bared his teeth like an angry squirrel and squeezed harder. She walloped the little man in the mouth. He stumbled backward and landed on the floor near his cane.

She shrieked and rushed to the door. He drew the sword and ran after her. She screamed hysterically, waving her hands as she made her way to the stairs. Reverend Real Estate dived, plunged the sword in, covered her gaping mouth with his hand, and together they rolled to the bottom of the stairs. They landed at Little Emma's feet, the schoolmarm wrapped in ribbons of blood.

Reverend Blasingame could barely catch his breath. "Heat the water . . ." he said, his belly rising and falling " . . . you've got cleaning to do."

Collingswood paced back and forth in his office, his hands clasped behind his back. He wanted to make a run for the Majestic Hotel, but was afraid he'd get a bullet in the back on the way.

He'd made a serious mistake getting involved with Reverend Real Estate, he realized now. He'd always thought the preacher slightly mad, but the man had become dangerous.

Collingswood looked out the window. What if he crawled out? Only a few feet, he'd be on State Street. The Majestic Hotel was a short distance away.

He stood beside the window, afraid to move. A killer might be waiting for him. The doorknob turned behind him, and he spun around. The door opened and revealed Runge, thumbs hooked in his gunbelt.

"Ain't plannin' to jump out that winder, was you, Mr. Businessman?"

"Of course not. I was just . . . ah . . . thinking."

Runge whipped out his gun. "You ain't foolin' nobody, Mr. Businessman."

Collingswood raised his hands. "Just a minute!"

Runge pulled the trigger. The gunshot reverberated through the house. Collingswood fell back, horror on his face, as the truth of life dawned on him. You can't make a pact with the devil, and hope to come out ahead.

Reverend Blasingame entered his office, carrying a slice of vanilla cake covered with thick white frosting. He sat at his desk, took out his tincture of laudanum with frantic ratlike movements, fixed himself a double dose. He raised the glass to his lips and drank it down in one gulp.

Then he dug his fork into the cake, and it became the withered breast of Abigail Thornton. Four dots of blood welled out, and the horror caught in his throat. He tried to breathe, his throat full of masticated cake and icing, but no air came. His tongue stuck out and he gagged, groping frantically in the air. He desperately needed air. He'd suffocate.

Something slammed into his back, forced him to cough, and a ball of sweet dough was expelled from his mouth. He gulped air, and turned to Little Emma.

"You all right, sir?"

His chest heaved with exertion, and his clerical collar was askew. He patted her head and said gratefully, "You're a good girl."

"Sheriff Wheatlock is here to see you."

Reverend Blasingame's eyes widened to saucers. "Did he say what he wanted? Have you cleaned up the blood? Hurry and finish!"

She left the room, and he glanced around, straightening articles that had been knocked over. He threw the dough into the wastebasket, adjusted his collar, took a deep breath, felt the laudanum taking hold. Everything was going to be all right. He heard the sheriff's steps on his stairs.

Sheriff Wheatlock looked at the inner sanctum of Reverend Blasingame. The only light came from the lantern on his desk, bulging bookcases lined the walls. Reverend Blasingame looked paler than usual.

"What can I do for you, Sheriff?"

"Some people complained 'bout screams comin' from this house. You hear somethin'?"

"Just the unrest in the street. A shot every now and then. It's not the quietest night we've ever had in Sundust, I'm afraid."

"You carry weight in this town, Reverend. I was wonderin' if you'd talk to the people, calm 'em down. Lots of 'em respect you. Might work."

Reverend Blasingame raised his hand like Christ in an old Russian icon. "Not good for a preacher to get mixed up in politics. God doesn't need more enemies than he's got already."

The gang from the Triangle Spur saddled their horses in the stable. A volley of shots erupted in the center of town. Koussivitsky opened the back door of the stable, and starlight came into view. They led their horses outside.

"Wait a minute," Stone said, glancing around. "Slipchuck's missing."

They looked at each other and realized it was true. The old stagecoach driver had vanished.

"I bet I know where he is," Cassandra said, a frown on her face. "We can't leave him behind."

A crowd of cowboys gathered in front of the bank, hollering obscenities. They held guns, bottles of whiskey, knives, torches, boulders, rocks, lengths of lumber.

A barrel-chested waddie stood before the bank doors. His name was Scroggins, he was half-drunk, and somehow he'd become leader of the mob.

"We come a long way!" he hollered. "We deserve better'n this!"

The cowboys in the crowd roared their agreement, and one threw a bottle at the bank's shuttered window.

"We din't ask to come here!" Scroggins continued. "Folks from this town rode out an' invited us in! Where's the money!"

The crowd took up the chant: "Where's the money! Where's the money!"

"I say we should take what's due us! Burn the son of a bitch to the ground!"

The crowd surged toward the bank. Scroggins aimed his six-gun at the lock.

"Hold it right there!" said Sheriff Wheatlock, pointing his gun at Scroggins. "Touch that lock, I'll shoot you where you stand!"

Scroggins couldn't back down now. He and the mob were drunker and more angry than last time, and harder to intimidate. If Sheriff Wheatlock could shoot the gun out of Scroggins's hand, he'd stop them, be a hero, maybe get a raise from the town council. He fired, a red smirch appeared on Scroggins's sleeve. Scroggins screamed in pain. The mob shouted a cacophony of disapproval, many of the cowboys drew their guns. Wheatlock stood his ground.

"Any man touches this bank, I'll shoot him down." The crooked sheriff was outnumbered, but not afraid.

The crowd stopped. They hadn't come all the way from Texas to get cheated out of their money. Wheatlock glared at them, no coward. The situation was tense, could explode any moment.

Then, out of the night, came the order: "At ease!" A major in the U.S. Army marched toward the bank. He wore his full dress uniform, sword at his side, pistol in a holster. Most of the cowboys had been soldiers, and relaxed in the middle of the street.

The major's campaign hat tilted at a rakish angle, medals covered his chest, he'd been from Bull Run to the Battle of the Washita, with numerous stops in between.

"My name is Major Salter!" he told them in a booming voice. "I'm ordering all of you to disperse in the name of the United States Government! Don't do anything tonight that you'll regret the rest of your lives!"

"Where's the money!"

"The train'll be here tomorrow afternoon! You'll get your money then!"

"What if the train don't come?"

Major Salter placed his fists on his waist. "If the train doesn't come, I'll help you burn the town down, because I want to get out of here myself!"

They cheered, threw hats into the air. "I want to buy that man a drink!" They hoisted Major Salter onto their shoulders, carried him toward the Bucket of Blood Saloon.

The wheel of fortune spun, the freak show went on. A new act had joined that day: Dr. Abner Wenders, dentist. A cowboy sat on the chair, mouth opened wide and eyes glistening fear. Dr. Wenders held a pliers in his hand, tried to pull the tooth out of the cowboy's mouth.

It wouldn't come, and Dr. Wenders yanked more energetically. He placed his knee in the cowboy's lap for greater leverage. The cowboy yawped like a wounded steer as his friends offered encouragement.

Dr. Wenders removed his pliers from the cowboy's mouth, and blood trickled down the cowboy's chin. A bottle was passed to the cowboy, and he guzzled down several swallows. He was trying to be a man, but the pain was horrific.

Dr. Wenders grasped the offending tooth with pliers, placed his free hand on the cowboy's hairy, bearded jaw, pulled the clamps tight, and tugged. He focused every ounce of energy in his body, just as they'd taught him at the Western Alabama College of Dental Arts. Something loosened in the cowboy's mouth. Dr. Wenders knew victory was in sight, and pulled again. There was a terrible crunching sound, the tooth broke loose. Dr. Wenders went flying backward, and the cowboys caught him. The patient passed out from whiskey and pain. Dr. Wenders waved the bloody tooth in the air. "Only two dollars! Pay yer money down!"

Outside the freak show tent, Slipchuck approached the old lady selling tickets. His hat was low over his face, so nobody would recognize him. He paid his money and went inside.

The sound of the hurdy-gurdy became louder. A group of gaily costumed midgets performed flip-flops in the air. The tattooed man delivered his lecture.

"I need ink," he said. "It's food for my blood." He flexed his tiny bicep muscles covered with a sailing ship. "Whenever I feel weak, I get me another tattoo."

"What happens when you got no more room?" a cowboy asked.

"Tattoo over the old ones."

Slipchuck passed behind the tattooed man. The object of his deepest desire drew closer. He stared at her incredible unimaginable breasts. She had the face of angel, a crown of auburn hair fell to her shoulders, and beneath it an enormous mass of flesh.

He walked toward her in a trance as she placed another spoonful of pudding into her bottomless mouth.

* * *

Runge and his gunfighters, guns drawn, entered the stable. They examined the brands on horses and didn't see any from the Triangle Spur.

"Flew the coop," Runge said. "Let's git after 'em."

He holstered his gun and moved toward his horse when a shadow moved behind a bale of hay. Runge slapped iron. The old stable manager moved into a shaft of moonlight, his hands in the air and beady eyes fixed on the gun barrel pointed at his chest.

"You see which way the crew from the Triangle Spur went?" Runge asked.

"Heard 'em say somethin' 'bout a-stoppin' by the carnival 'fore they pulled out."

A faint smile cracked Runge's tiny vulpine face. "This looks like it, boys. We got 'em where we want 'em now."

Major Salter wobbled slightly as he made his way down the corridor to his hotel room. One free drink had led to another. He'd saved the town from bloodshed, nothing was too good for him.

He came to the door of his room, and hesitated to knock. He was a husband coming home late, smelling of drink, expecting to get nagged. He'd rather face an angry mob than his angry wife.

He took a deep breath, squared his shoulders, raised his fist, knocked. The door opened, and his wife wore a yellow silk dressing gown that showed the outlines of her nipples. "I saw the whole thing from the window," she said. "You were wonderful. I'm so proud I married you."

Major Salter was dazed as her lips touched his. He nearly tripped over his sword as she dragged him toward the bed.

Slipchuck stood before the fat lady, who nibbled the drumstick of a chicken. "I remember you," she said, "the little man who snuck into my tent while I slept. That wasn't a nice thing to do."

"Meant no harm," Slipchuck said. "I done it for love." He gazed into her eyes, hoping to ignite a fire with his mad passion. "I might not look like much," he admitted, "I could never give you what you want, but just let me look at you fer a while longer, 'fore I leave and we never see each other again."

Slipchuck heard a footfall behind him, spun around, drew his Colt. The tattooed man stood there, naked but for his loincloth. Both men aimed loaded weapons at each other.

The tattooed man was surprised by Slipchuck's fighting stance. "Stay away from my wife," he stuttered.

"Drop that gun," Slipchuck told him. "You can catch me once, but you'll never do it again."

The tattooed man had never been in a showdown before, a terrifying prospect. He dropped the gun to the ground. Slipchuck picked it up, jammed it into his belt. Then he turned to the fat lady.

"I could fight fer you," he said. "I ain't afraid of nothin'."

"I love my husband," she replied. "Go away."

Slipchuck looked like he'd been trampled by a stompede. He dragged his feet toward the dark shadows, gun in hand. If he couldn't have her, he didn't want to live. He raised the barrel to his head.

A hand clamped on his wrist. John Stone towered above him. "What you think you're doing, pard?"

Cassandra said, "We've got work to do, and you're holding us up. Let's be on our way."

The fat lady made a little wave. The love of his life had dismissed him for a plate of mashed potatoes. Slipchuck followed the others toward the tent's exit. The other feller always gits the pretty gals.

They emerged from the tent, walked toward the horses. Stone placed his arm around Cassandra's waist. "We'll get married in Abilene. In a real church with a decent pastor, not Reverend Real Estate."

Moonlight shone on his fine profile. He had nobility when he was sober. Why couldn't he be this way all the time? "I wouldn't marry you unless you promised to stay away from whiskey."

"Even at the big party?"

"You can have the party, but after it's over, nothing for thirty days. Then I'll marry you, if you still want to."

Stone had the weird sense that he was shaking the firm grip of Duke Truscott. Slipchuck slouched, a defeated man. He'd caught a glimpse of ecstasy, but it wasn't meant to be.

Manolo, the Mexican knife fighter, placed his arm around Slipchuck's shoulders. "Do not be unhappy, amigo. A thing like this happens to every man. You come to Mexico with me, you like fat girls. I know a whole village of them near Vera Cruz. They walk like this."

He stuck his belly out and waddled like the fat lady. Even Cassandra had to laugh. The ears of the horses were pricked up, they looked toward the carnival. Stone spun around, couldn't see anything.

"Something's out there," he said. "Horses're spooked."

They searched the night, saw only shadows among tents. "Let's get out of here," Cassandra said. "This place is giving me the willies."

The night filled with thunder and lightning. Cowboys, vaqueros, and Cassandra dived to the ground. The barrage of gunfire exploded into the ground all around them.

The military part of Stone's brain clicked on. He weighed the options and didn't have all night to come up with the answer. If they made a run for the horses they'd be cut down.

Bullets peppered the ground, but they were difficult targets lying flat in the moonlight. Moose Roykins tried to bandage his left arm with a torn length of shirt. "Bastards got me!" he said through clenched teeth.

Midgets, freaks, clowns, and dancing girls ran in all directions, screaming. The old lion roared mightily in his cage, and the tattooed man escorted his immense wife to safety behind a wagon. Stone saw a comet passing through the sky overhead. He dived through the air, caught the bound sticks of dynamite in his hands.

The fuse sizzled angrily, he reared back his arm. A bullet creased his left ear, he hurled the packet with all his strength. It arched into the sky, terrific explosion, tents blown to smithereens. Stone was on his feet in a second. "Let's get the hell out of here!"

Koussivitsky hollered the battle cry of the Don Cossacks. All the others rushed behind him. Muzzle blasts dotted the stand of trees to their left. Stone dived into the grass again. Bullets stitched into the ground in front of his nose. They had to get the rifles and shotgun. He tensed for a run at the horses, when two more bundles of dynamite came looping lazily through the autumn night.

Stone leapt into the air, while Don Emilio reached for the explosives on his side. A bullet shot through Don Emilio's thigh, but he held steady and threw the dynamite back. Then he fell to the ground as if someone had rammed a red-hot poker into his leg. He rolled over, cursed in Spanish. Stone heaved his dynamite, then dropped down again.

The explosives detonated among the tents, bodies blew into the air. It was war, and Stone felt that old rush of juice. He reached toward his belt for his sword, but only his empty holster was there.

"Let's get out of here!"

"I cannot move!" Don Emilio replied, his Mexican vaquero pants drenched with blood.

Stone ran toward him, picked him off the ground.

"You will never make it with me," Don Emilio said. "Leave me behind."

"You're coming with us whether you like it or not!"

Don Emilio weighed one hundred ninety pounds, and Stone tipped the scales at two-forty. Stone ran slower than the rest, but he steadily made his way toward the horses. The enemy wasn't firing anymore. It looked like they'd get away.

A new voice resounded in the night. "Hold it right there! This is Major Salter of the Seventh Cavalry! Drop your guns and put your hands in the air!"

An officer in blue held a sword in one hand and a gun in the other as he led a horde of armed townspeople up the hill. "We were about to ride out of here," Stone said, "and somebody in those tents fired at us."

Don Emilio's eyes were like raging infernos. "I ever find who they are . . ."

"Heard the explosions in town," the officer said, and Stone noticed half his buttons were undone. "My name's Salter."

"John Stone."

Cassandra stepped forward. "He works for me. I suggest you put this town under martial law immediately."

Major Salter had spent most of the day in bed with a woman, but that didn't prevent him from admiring another woman. "Any of your people hurt?"

"Over here," said Slipchuck, illuminated by torches held by townspeople. Manolo lay at his feet, a bullet through his chest. "Nothing you can do for him," Slipchuck said. "He's daid."

Everyone stared at Manolo, knife fighter and brutal killer, but good *compañero* across many hard miles.

Major Salters noticed Stone's hat. "What outfit were you with?"

"Wade Hampton."

"Wesley Merrit."

They shook hands for the first time. A man with a pug nose and freckles stepped forward. "Captain Lewton Rooney, also of the Hampton Brigade."

It was the officer corps gathering in the midst of the crowd, and they were joined by Captain Koussivitsky of the Don Cossacks, a strange military brotherhood among men who hardly knew each other.

They examined the area in the torchlight. Dead men lay on the ground, and the wounded groaned. Stone kneeled next to one of them. "Who put you up to this?"

"Go to hell," the man said through clenched teeth, guts spilling out of his stomach. Stone admired his loyalty, but would've preferred a traitor.

"Over here!" shouted Slipchuck.

He was perched on his hands and knees, looking at the ground, while beside him stood a cowboy with a torch. "One of 'em come this way."

The torches illuminated drops of blood on the grass. Stone got on his knees and examined it. Slipchuck had been giving him tracking lessons, and he noted how the grass was bent back, direction of the blood trail. It led toward town.

Slipchuck drew his gun and looked toward the sparkling lights of Sundust. "We foller this trail," he said, "we'll find the varmints what shot me amigo."

8

REVEREND BLASINGAME SLEPT on the sofa in his office, dreaming of the hottest regions of hell, where imps with forked tails shoveled coal into raging fires, and sinners roasted on slowly turning spits.

The stink was rotten eggs, screams of agony hurt his eardrums. He ran among red-hot coals, as rivers of boiling water streamed past him, and belches of pestiferous steam assailed his nostrils.

A tidal wave of molten lava rolled toward him, bubbling and seething. A little red demon raised his head out of it and shrieked. The heat set Reverend Real Estate's clothes on fire, he tried desperately to move his feet, but they were glued to the ground. Somebody shook his shoulder.

He opened his eyes, and it was Little Emma. "Sir . . . terrible . . . a man . . . downstairs . . ."

Reverend Blasingame reached for his cane. "Is he armed?"

"He's dying . . ."

Reverend Blasingame jumped out of bed, his heart chugging in his chest. Everything was going wrong, his life disintegrating, one crisis after another. He ran quick as his short legs could take him down the stairs, saw a man slumped in a chair beside the kitchen table. Emma appeared behind Reverend Blasingame, and she held the lantern in her hand. It illuminated Trevino with his arms wrapped around his chest. His hands and the front of his shirt were drenched with blood.

123

Reverend Blasingame knelt in front of him. "What happened?"

Trevino opened his mouth, but no sound came. His eyes went glassy, and he leaned forward. Reverend Blasingame tried to get out of the way, but he was a roly-poly little man. Trevino fell on top of him.

Reverend Blasingame squirmed away, covered with Trevino's blood. He rose to his feet, and a wave of panic overtook him. His eyes darted excitedly about the room, searching for a solution.

Little Emma peered out the window. "People comin'!"

He rushed toward the window. A crowd carrying torches and guns approached the rectory. With Abigail's corpse in the root cellar, Reverend Real Estate's worst dream was coming true. He had to pull himself together and *do something*.

In the extremity of his deep anxiety, he had a vision. He was being presented with the ultimate test of his faith. His moment of doubt and shame passed. A smile came over his face. Of course.

The crowd gathered behind the rectory. Slipchuck squinted at the ground. "Went right in that door," he said.

Major Salter looked at the church building, and a wave of foreboding came over him. Preachers belonged to organizations with offices in Washington.

"What you waitin' fer?" Slipchuck asked. "I told you where he went!"

Major Salter's career would be over if he made one wrong move now. "I think we should get the sheriff in on this. Don't want to overstep my authority."

Mayor McGillicuddy stepped out of the crowd, followed by Alderman Shaeffer. "We're elected officials," he said. "I think we ought to search that house!"

"Now just a minute!" hollered Hudspeth, armed with a shotgun. "You can't go bustin' in on Reverend Blasingame like he was a common criminal."

Slipchuck pointed to the blood on the ground. "It's where the trail leads."

"It's the house of God, and we dare not desecrate it!"

Mayor McGillicuddy said, "We have reason to believe a

bushwhacker is holed up in there." He turned to Major Salter. "Break down the door!"

"Like hell you will!" Hudspeth leveled his gun at Major Salter. "I'm a deacon of this church, and you're not breakin' down no doors!"

Major Salter saw the crowd break apart into two factions, each facing each other across the courtyard. The crew from the Triangle Spur stood near the door. "One of my men's been killed," Stone said in his deep cavalry officer's voice, "and two more wounded in a bushwhack. The blood leads to this door. We're going in." He aimed his gun at the doorknob.

The townspeople looked at the trail-hardened cowboys and vaqueros, and nobody dared challenge them. Stone cocked the hammer of his gun, and Koussivitsky stood beside him, ready to throw his colossal shoulder at the door. As Stone squeezed the trigger, suddenly the knob turned. The door opened, Reverend Blasingame stood before him, lantern in hand, black shirt and white clerical collar bloody.

Stone lowered his gun and eased back the hammer. Reverend Blasingame's white hair was mussed, and his eyes had a peculiar gleam.

"This way, gentlemen," he said.

They followed him into the kitchen, and on the floor, next to the table, lay Trevino in a pool of blood. Cowboys and townspeople strained to see, and Little Emma stood in the shadows of the next room, observing silently.

"I was in my study," Reverend Blasingame explained, his voice the epitome of calm reason, "working on my Sunday sermon, when there was a knock on the door. My housekeeper opened up, and this poor unfortunate fellow asked for me. I came downstairs, and it was clear he was mortally wounded. He asked me to pray for him, and I did." Reverend Blasingame gazed sadly at the blood on his clothing. "He died in my arms."

There was silence in the room. Many were deeply moved by the pastor's story; others appeared skeptical.

"Search the place," Stone said. "There may be more."

Hudspeth made a threatening motion with his rifle, but Stone snapped his gun on him. "One of my men was killed, and the people who did it are going to pay."

"The reverend just told you the man on the floor was the only one who came here. Don't you believe him?"

"Hell no."

A cold glimmer of hatred appeared in Reverend Blasingame's eyes.

Hudspeth said, "This is a sanctuary of God. You desecrate it, there'll be war in this town, you mark my words."

Major Salter stepped between them. "Gentlemen, please . . ."

Mayor McGillicuddy took a notepad out of his pocket. "I'll write out the search warrant right here and now."

"You'd better write your death warrant while you're at it," Hudspeth said.

It looked like a shootout in the dim light of a small crowded room. "I think," Major Salter said, "we'd all better step outside and get some fresh air. Talk this over like reasonable men."

"You can talk all you want," Hudspeth said, "you ain't searchin' the reverend's house."

"Yes we are," Stone replied. "Nobody shoots at me and gets away with it."

"This is the house of God!"

Lewton Rooney stepped forward. "Everybody knows Reverend Real Estate is behind every dirty deal in this town. I say search the building immediately."

Men pointed guns at each other at close quarters. Major Salter thought of his beautiful wife as a merry widow.

"There's a dead woman in the cellar," Slipchuck said.

His voice went like lightning through the room. Everyone turned to him, and he stood in a doorway, Colt in hand.

"We'd better take a look," Mayor McGillicuddy said.

Slipchuck led them through the corridor and down the rough-hewn wooden stairs to the cellar. She lay on a worktable, her complexion white, a faint sickly sweet odor arose from her corpse.

"It's the schoolmarm!"

They gathered around. She'd been stabbed repeatedly, her face wrenched in agony.

"Clear-cut case of murder," Mayor McGillicuddy said. "Where's the preacher?"

They looked around. The pastor of the Mount Zion Church of God was nowhere to be seen.

• • •

He ran through the back alleys of Sundust, a plump figure in a black shirt and clerical collar smudged with the blood of a gunfighter. He wore no hat, a wild frightened look was in his eyes, he feared the wrath of God.

He came to the end of an alley, peered both ways, saw a drunken cowboy passed out in a backyard, lying on his face. Somebody hollered on the main street of town. If they caught him, they'd hang him high. He felt a sudden constriction in his chest. It felt as though the Apocalypse had come to pass in his life.

He needed sanctuary, ran out of the shadows and crossed the yard, passed sheds and privies. A mongrel dog rushed from behind a woodpile and snapped at his heels as he fled toward the outskirts of town.

He came to a small boarded-up nondescript shack near the stockyards. It looked as though it was ready to fall over, and an old FOR RENT sign was badly faded. Reverend Blasingame could smell the cattle in their pens; the moon sat near the top of a lone cottonwood tree. He grit his teeth and jammed the key into the lock, opened the door. Quickly he jumped inside and shut the door behind him.

He was assailed by stale odors, walked into a cobweb. A spider crawled on his face, and he frantically clawed it away. He tripped over a chair, fell to the floor. A cloud of dust arose in the air. He hadn't been here for a long time, in fact had nearly forgotten the place. He'd designed it himself in the early days when the town was being built, in case he needed a quick hideout.

It was cheaply constructed, a dwelling poor people rented, the outdoors could be seen through cracks in the boards that covered the windows. He didn't dare light a candle. But he was safe.

A cot was pushed against the wall, he sat upon it. He loosened his clerical collar and breathed deeply. Against the other wall were jugs of water, crates of food, clothing, guns, laudanum, and saddlebags full of gold. Grow a beard, change his appearance. One dark night steal a horse and ride away.

This was his first chance to think, he was deeply shaken. Was he a false prophet? He remembered his Bible:

His eyes were a flame of fire, and on his head were many crowns . . .

That day in the fields had been no dream. God had spoken to him. To doubt that would be to doubt his sanity. What did God want from him?

Babylon the great is fallen, and is become the habitation of devils, and the hold of every foul spirit, and a cage of every unclean and hateful bird.

"You want me to destroy Sundust?" he asked. "How can I do that? I don't have anything!" If he showed his face outside, he could be shot on sight. You couldn't expect ordinary men to understand a dead schoolmarm in the cellar.

. . . if a man has faith the size of a mustard-seed, he can move mountains.

There's a deeper significance I don't understand. His eyes fell on a crate of tinned beef and another of hardtack. A good meal clarified a man's thinking. *At least I won't starve,* he thought, prying up wooden slats.

The front desk in the lobby of the Majestic Hotel was surrounded by homeless freaks, midgets, and clowns clamoring for rooms.

"Only two rooms left," the room clerk told them. "You'll all have to make the best of it."

"I need at least one room just for myself!" said the fat lady.

He couldn't disagree. "Might be able to find space in the attic."

"What about the lobby?" asked Dr. Wenders.

"Twenty-five cents a night," the room clerk replied.

Slipchuck's eyes fell on the fat lady arguing with the room clerk. He swerved toward her, but Duvall grabbed him by the scruff of his neck.

"Keep movin', you goddamned idiot."

Slipchuck tried to break loose, but Duvall's grip was like

steel. Duvall half pushed and half carried Slipchuck to the stairs, and they climbed to the third floor. They made their way down the hall, and Slipchuck unlocked the door.

They entered Cassandra's room, could smell her perfume. Slipchuck lit the lantern, and they saw her clothes in the closet. Duvall looked through the window at the main street of town, and it was nearly deserted. The excitement was over, everyone gone to bed.

The rest of the crew was spending the night at Rooney's house. Tomorrow the herd would be sold. The drive was finally over and the party could begin. Slipchuck reached into his saddlebags and pulled out his old battered deck of cards.

"Cut you fer the bed," he said.

They cut, turned the faces up. Slipchuck had the king of hearts, no one else was close. They took off their boots, putrid fragrance filled the room. Duvall opened the windows. They felt cramped after so many nights on the plains.

"See you all in the mornin'," Slipchuck said. He crawled into bed and placed his Colt underneath the pillow. The mattress was soft as a cloud, he smiled as he sank into it. The other men lay on the floor, bones jutting hard wood. They looked up and saw whitewashed ceiling instead of the moon and stars.

The bed jiggled for several moments every time Slipchuck moved. He tossed and turned like a cork on the ocean. Squeaky, creaky sounds filled the room.

"Be still!" somebody growled.

Slipchuck felt as though he were drowning in marshmallow. Never really liked beds that much. He climbed out and joined the others on the floor.

It was hard and painful. The ground at least had a little give, and you sweep together a few leaves, you got a nice bed for the night. A gun was fired outside, and everybody in the room jumped three inches off the floor.

Pedro looked out the window, Colt in hand. "Are you thinking what I am thinking, amigos?"

"Let's get out of here," Duvall replied. "Damn place probably's got fleas."

●　●　●

Cassandra and Stone lay naked in bed, and the cool prairie breeze wafted through the open window. He held her closely, nuzzled her fragrant golden hair. He loved the feel of her body against his.

"I'm tired of fighting," she mused aloud. "All I want is peace and quiet. What do you think you're doing?"

"You know very well what I'm doing."

There was silence for a few moments, then she said, "Lew is in the next room."

"We don't have to be noisy."

It was three o'clock in the morning, and a tall, lean figure walked the dirt sidewalk of Main Street, a black cape wrapped around him, a slouch hat covering most of his face.

The tattooed man only came out at night, when people couldn't see him; he caused a disturbance in broad daylight. Not many men wore the tattoo of a cobra on their foreheads, sailing ships on their cheeks. The tattooed life forced him into a strange clandestine existence not without its charms. The town was peaceful at night, after such a tumultuous day.

He was now president of the carnival, and many worries bent his shoulders. Where would they buy new tents? Another act was needed to replace Koussivitsky. The dancing girls wanted to run off with cowboys. The musicians wanted to become ranchers. His wife demanded star billing. Every walk of life has its own special torments and afflictions.

Something moved near the doorway of a saloon. At first the tattooed man thought it was a dog, but it was a little person, one of the bunch from the carnival out for a walk.

The tattooed man bent lower, saw a misshapen hunchback girl, her face covered with a scarf. Shyly she raised the palm of her small hand for a few coins. The tattooed man had sharp eyes and took in every item of her appearance. She wasn't with the carnival.

"Who are you?" he asked.

"Emma."

"You have no place to live, Emma?"

She shook her head. Her eyes were red from crying. "Let me show you something, Emma." He took a step backward, entered the light emanating from the saloon. Dramatically he opened his cape, she saw the dog on his chin, flag on his chest, diamonds and rubies around his throat. He covered himself again and dropped to one knee in front of her. "Are you hungry?"

She nodded.

"Come with me, and you'll meet my lovely wife."

Little Emma hesitated, then offered her hand. He took it, gave a little squeeze. "We'll be good friends," he said. "You'll see things you never seen before."

They walked down the street, passing darkened storefronts. Most of the saloons were quiet, a few men sitting at tables, others passed out at the bar.

They came to the Majestic Hotel. Strange shapes slept on the floor of the lobby. The tattooed man pulled her gently. "You can meet them tomorrow."

They climbed the stairs, he inserted his key in a lock. The door opened, and Little Emma walked into a small hotel room. The lantern burned next to the bed, illuminating a gigantic woman with the face of a fairy queen. The queen turned to her, stared for a few moments, and Little Emma felt sure she'd be kicked down the stairs at any moment.

"Come closer, dear," the queen said.

Emma hesitated, but the tattooed man pushed her forward. She took little pigeon-toed steps closer to the bed.

"Pull away the scarf," the queen said. "Don't be afraid. I won't bite you."

Emma's hand trembled as she lowered the scarf.

The fat lady saw the nonexistent nose, twisted mouth, eyes out of balance. "The best beauty of all," she said, "comes from inside a person, and what a pretty little girl you are. Come up on the bed with me, dear, and we'll have cookies and milk."

A broad smile wreathed Little Emma's face as she moved toward the soft immense arms of the fairy queen.

Reverend Real Estate sat on his bed, cracking nuts and stuffing the meat into his mouth. He couldn't sleep, had a headache, felt afraid. How did twenty of the meanest gunmen in Kansas get beat by a scraggly crew of drunken cowboys? Cassandra

Whiteside was a witch, that was clear to him now. She'd put a spell on him, opened him to lust and false pride.

Women twist men's minds. Perhaps that's what God was telling him. He'd given in to the temptation of Eve, was cast naked into the world. He poured himself a strong dose of laudanum, drank it down. Cows mooed in the distance; it was almost daylight. Somehow he had to survive a few days in this hellhole, but he was at peace with himself. He knew what God wanted now. Sundust must be destroyed, like Sodom and Gomorrah, and Cassandra Whiteside must die.

9

STONE EXAMINED HIS freshly washed face in the mirror. Lines had deepened around his mouth and eyes, and he was amazed at the beating he'd taken over the years. A cynical man looked back at him, not the happy-go-lucky kid of days gone by.

He wiped water from his face, noticed the door ajar to Rooney's office. The wall behind the desk was covered with books, and Stone hadn't browsed through a library for years. He entered the empty office and looked at the bookcases. An old beat-up leather-bound antique caught his eye, ratty and out of place beside distinguished tomes on law, agriculture, and modern business practices.

He reached up and took it down. It felt familiar in his hands. The signature *Ashley Tredegar* was written inside the front cover. Now he remembered. It had been Ashley's copy of *The Iliad*. Many times during the war Stone had browsed through it while Ashley was busy elsewhere. His favorite passage was in the Twenty-first Book. He flipped through the pages. It took moments to find the passage:

> *What a man I am, how huge, how splendid. Yet even I have also my death and my strong destiny. There shall be a dawn or an afternoon or a noontime when some warrior in the fighting will take the life from me also.*

Spoken by Achilles before he slew Lyaon on the field of battle, it summarized the truth of war to Stone. Sooner or later a soldier is killed. You have to accept it, and get on with your job.

One night in San Antone he'd wandered drunk into a fortune-teller's parlor, and she'd predicted he'd die young. At first he thought she was just another charlatan, but she also said Calvin Blakemore would die young too, and Blakemore had been gunned down by rustlers a few weeks later.

Stone had been extra cautious after Blakemore's funeral, but nothing happened and he gradually thought less about the Gypsy's curse. It was coincidence, superstition, bullshit, but troubled him anyway.

Rooney entered the office. "Had to run out for a few minutes," he explained, pug nose red from exertion. "What you got there? Oh. I was the one assigned to collect Ashley's personal belongings, and I kept it to remember him by. Didn't think anyone would care." Rooney darted his fingers into his back pockets and looked out the window. "I've had it all these years, and you were a closer friend of his than I. Maybe you should take it for a while."

"I'd lose it."

Cassandra walked into the room. "The funeral is in fifteen minutes, and you're not even dressed!"

She looked like the avenging angel, and Stone fled beneath her merciless glare. Cassandra turned to Rooney, and he was already halfway out the back door. She hitched up her gunbelt in the manner of Duke Truscott and walked to the kitchen for another cup of thick black coffee, just the way Truscott liked it.

Tod Buckalew approached the Mount Zion Church of God. He climbed down from his horse, threw the reins over the rail behind the rectory, knocked on the rear door, waited for Little Emma to open up. She didn't come. He reached toward the knob, the door opened. He looked inside the darkened kitchen. A shotgun was pointed at Buckalew's shirt.

Buckalew stopped cold in his tracks. Sheriff Wheatlock chewed the butt of a cigar. "What you doing here?" Buckalew asked.

"Thought I might ask you the same thing," the sheriff replied.

"I'm here to see the reverend."

"He's wanted for murder."

It often happened to Buckalew, the world became unreal, impossible, fantastical. "What you talkin' about?"

"Knifed the schoolmarm. Found her in his cellar. Where you been, boy? How come you don't know what's been goin' on?"

"Took me a little ride. Why'd he do it?"

"Din't hang around long enough to tell us. We're offerin' one thousand dollars reward for him, dead or alive. You wouldn't know where he is, would you, Buckalew?" Sheriff Wheatlock looked at him skeptically, one eye cocked.

"I thought you was on his payroll too, Wheatlock."

"Now just a minute . . ."

"They say you're the best sheriff money can buy."

"Reverend Real Estate's wanted for murder, that's all I know."

"Point that shotgun some other way."

"Point it where I want."

They faced each other across the kitchen floor. Sheriff Wheatlock had the drop on him, but there'd be other days. Buckalew backed toward the door, made his friendly smile. "Nice seein' you again, Sheriff. Look forward to next time."

Marcus Strickland entered Mayor McGillicuddy's office. "Like to speak with you."

The mayor of Sundust looked up from the letter he was writing to the governor. "Good thing you dropped by, Marcus. Intended to put out a warrant for your arrest. You're in up to your neck with Reverend Real Estate, isn't that so?"

"That's what I came here about." Strickland's eyes were bloodshot from lack of sleep. "He told me to close the bank yesterday, and I followed orders. He owns it, I'm only his employee. Don't blame the mess on me."

Mayor McGillicuddy leaned forward and looked into Strickland's eyes. "In other words, the bank was never out of money?"

"Enough money in the vault to handle any transaction."

"There'll be a complete investigation, but in the meantime I suggest you open up the bank for business. Maybe, just maybe, we can save this town."

The casket was a rectangular oak planked box, and it sat on a pile of dirt. Reverend Tipps stood behind the casket, Bible in hand.

"He was a loyal friend," Reverend Tipps said. "Many a time he . . ."

His voice pealed across Boot Hill, merged with the hoot and moo of cattle loading onto boxcars on the other side of town. Cassandra raised her eyes and discreetly looked at her men, some of the vaqueros cried openly. They'd been in many a cantina with Manolo, shared hardships, now he was gone.

Her eyes fell on big John Stone, head bowed and hat in his hands. Taller than the others, broad-shouldered, the sun gleamed on his wavy hair.

She'd seen Manolo kill another vaquero once, yet he'd been the campfire comedian every night, always respectful toward *La Señora*. Manolo had family near Guadalajara, she'd send his pay to them. The bank was scheduled to open that morning, and she'd sell the herd to Rooney after the funeral. The drive was finally over, and she hoped the killing had ended. What more could possibly happen?

Blasingame sat at the table in his hideout shack, examining his weaponry in the dim light that peeked through cracks in the boarded-up windows. He had a Sharps buffalo gun, a Colt Police pistol with two boxes of .36-caliber cartridges, and a Hammond Bulldog Derringer with a box of .44-caliber loads. They'd never take him alive.

He heard a knock at the door. His heart thumped loudly in his chest.

"Daddy?"

Blasingame threw the bolt and opened the door. Buckalew slipped into the shack. Father and son stood in the middle of the floor.

"You were right, Dad," Buckalew said. He turned to the side, tensed, and whipped out his gun. "See? It's all the same body, just like you said. I'm fast as I ever was."

Reverend Blasingame couldn't believe his good fortune. He embraced the son he'd abandoned so long ago. "My boy, so good to see you again. I need your help desperately."

"Went to the rectory," Buckalew said, "and the sheriff was there. Told me you killed the schoolmarm."

He looked like a punctured balloon. "Had to do it."

They heard children's voices, moved toward a crack, looked outside. Little boys chased each other with wooden guns.

"Dangerous here," Blasingame said. "We've got to get away."

"What happened to the crew?"

"They bushwhacked the Triangle Spur, got the stuffing knocked out of them. Trevino showed up gutshot in my kitchen, but he died before he could tell me anything. You're the first person I've seen since then."

"There's lots more boys at the farms and ranches, Dad. We can pull 'em together, teach this town a lesson."

Blasingame smiled for the first time since coming to the shack. He touched the palm of his hand to his son's stubbled cheek. "My boy, it's so good to see you again."

Frank Quarternight rode the main street of Sundust, wearing a Mexican serape that concealed his hook. He was covered with dust, a thick black growth of stubble wreathed his chubby jowls. A crowd gathered in front of the bank, someone fired a gun. Another man stood in front of the bank, giving a speech.

Quarternight wasn't interested in speeches. The only thing that mattered was the next fast draw. He rode his horse into the stable, climbed down. An elderly man stepped out of the shadows. "He'p you, sir?"

"Stable my horse."

The stable master told him prices, and they struck a deal. Quarternight pulled down his blanket roll and saddlebags with one hand. "Triangle Spur in town?"

The stable master pointed. "Horses're over there."

Quarternight walked toward the horses from the Triangle Spur, and they pricked up their ears. They'd become nearly wild during the drive, and weren't accustomed to stables, clean straw, plenty of oats. Quarternight looked at them, and wondered which was John Stone's. You could tell a lot about a man from the way he maintained his mount.

Quarternight walked out of the stable, carrying his bedroll and saddlebags. He searched for a tall man who fit John Stone's description, saw several. A cheer went up, crowds rushed toward the door of the bank. A man never knew what he'd see when he came to a new town.

He entered the lobby of the Majestic Hotel, crossed to the desk. "Room for the night."

He paid, got his key, did everything with his right hand, kept his hook hidden. "Anybody from the Triangle Spur in this hotel?"

"A few."

"What room?"

"Two thirteen."

Quarternight hoisted his blanket roll and saddlebags, carried them up the stairs. He entered his room, like a million other hotel rooms, initials carved into the walls, sagging mattress, plank floors.

He was exhausted, head hurt, stomach ached, butt chaffed from hours in the saddle. He should take a bath, but was too tired. All he wanted to do was sleep. He tossed his hat onto the dresser, sat on the bed, pulled off his boots. Then he lay back, his Smith & Wesson in his hand.

He fell asleep almost instantaneously, and the girl in the bloody dress arose at the foot of his bed. She resumed her dance, waving her arms, leaning backward and kicking her leg in the air, her laughter ringing through Frank Quarternight's morbid dreams.

Lewton Rooney read the contract one last time. Cassandra and John Stone sat in front of him in his office, and the morning had become gray. Rooney finished reading the contract and passed it to Cassandra.

She examined it carefully. Twenty dollars a head, the going rate for mixed longhorns. Half the money paid after signing the contract, the rest when Rooney took possession of the herd. She picked up the pen and scratched her name at the bottom. The drive had finally come to an end.

Buckalew lay fast asleep. A narrow shaft of light illuminated his face, and Reverend Blasingame examined his son's profile, looking for traces of himself.

How ironic that this boy had returned to deliver him from his enemies. He hadn't cared about Buckalew when he'd been born, and less about his mother. There was no way of knowing for sure it was his own son. The mother slept with many men. It was her livelihood. Blasingame had been her fancy man for a brief time.

So the little bastard came back, and his gunhand was better than ever. Blasingame sat before the map he'd drawn of Sundust. His plan was to level the town and massacre every man.

The boys would strike in the first light of dawn, destroy everything. And then he'd build New Jerusalem out of the ashes, bigger and better than ever.

Inside the bank, tellers signed documents, counted money, pushed it forward. Cassandra withdrew an amount to cover expenses for several days, placed the coins in her saddlebags. Stone carried the heavy treasure outside, accompanied by Rooney. The other cowboys and vaqueros from the Triangle Spur had returned to the herd, to move it to the pens. Stone looked across the street at the Peacock Saloon. "Let's have a drink."

"Can't," Rooney replied. "Got to go to the stockyards and make arrangements for the herd. Catch up with you later in the day."

He walked away, leaving Stone and Cassandra in front of a Chinese laundry.

"Please don't get drunk," she said.

"Just a couple," Stone replied. "Why can't you come with me? Let's celebrate, you and me."

"I want to buy some clothes, the kind a woman would wear. Promise me you won't get drunk?"

"Sure."

They touched lips, he handed her the saddlebags, she headed toward the nearest store. He turned to the Sagebrush Saloon. A sign caught his eye: JEWELRY.

He remembered Marie's picture, saw flashing trinkets in the window. Mr. Peabody looked up from the watch he was fixing.

"Got my frame fixed?" Stone asked, scanning shelves covered with clocks ticking merrily.

Peabody reached behind him and produced it, frame straightened, shining dully in the dreary afternoon. "A woman came in and claimed to know your friend here."

Stone's heart stopped beating. His jaw dropped open. A great void opened before him. Slowly, with great deliberation, he said, "Where is the woman now?"

"Majestic Hotel, I imagine. She's Major Salter's wife." Peabody searched through his notepaper and found the document he wanted. "Said the woman in your picture is at Fort Hays."

Stone paid for the repairs, buttoned the picture into his shirt pocket, left the jewelry shop. He ran to the Majestic Hotel, advanced toward the front desk.

"What room is Major Salter in?"

The clerk told him, Stone vaulted up the stairs three at a time. He moved down the hall like a wildcat, found the door, knocked.

Footsteps came to him from the other side. He tensed, the door opened, and Major Salter stood there, hair mussed, wearing his robe, an enormous red mark on his neck where his wife had got carried away.

"Sorry to bother you," Stone said breathlessly, and he held up Marie's picture. "Your wife told the jeweler she knows this woman. Is your wife here now?"

Stone's face was flecked with consternation, his eyes darted about nervously. Major Salter placed his arm around Stone's shoulders. "Come in, have a drink with me and the missus."

Stone entered the room, and a slender, dark-tressed woman in a thin yellow silk robe stood beside the bed. He held the picture up to her. "You know this woman?"

"I've seen her face nearly every day for the past year."

Stone stared at her. Major Salter handed him a glass of whiskey, and Stone drank it in one gulp. Major Salter maneuvered Stone to a chair. It was a dream, he'd wake near the campfire with the cowboys and vaqueros of the Triangle Spur.

They sat on the sofa opposite him. Dorothy Salter said, "What do you want to know about her?"

"How is she?" he blurted. "What's she like? What does she do?"

"She's the wife of Major Scanlon, the provost marshal. I didn't like her, I'm sorry to say. Thought she was better than the rest of us, because her father used to own a plantation. It was disgraceful the way she treated that man she married!"

Major Scanlon placed his hand on his wife's knee. "Don't go overboard, dear. She wasn't that bad."

"Not to you, because she always played up to the men. I know a little flirt when I see one."

Stone held out his glass, and Major Salter refilled it. "When was the last time you saw her?" Stone asked.

" 'Bout a week ago, when we left Fort Hays," Mrs. Salter replied. "What's she to you?"

"We were engaged to be married." Stone told them about returning home from the war, she'd disappeared. "I've been looking for her ever since. Did she ever mention . . . me?"

Major Salter and his wife looked at each other. "No," they said in unison.

Stone was confused. He'd promised to marry Cassandra Whiteside, and Marie was at Fort Hays?

"She's turned that poor Major Scanlon into a drunkard," Mrs. Salter continued. "You can hear her screaming at him all over the post. Nothing he ever does is right."

Major Salter explained, "My wife and Mrs. Scanlon had a few donnybrooks, I want you to know. The nearest thing I can compare it to would be a knife fight, except they did it all with words."

Stone walked across the lobby of the Majestic Hotel, head spinning. He needed to sit down, the Peacock was a few doors down. Just when he'd given up the search for Marie, and was going to settle down peacefully with Cassandra Whiteside, Marie had to pop up.

He entered the saloon, made a beeline for the bar. It was late afternoon, thunder could be heard in the distance. The bartender moved toward him.

"Whiskey."

The glass was filled. Stone carried it to a table in the corner and blew out the candle. He sat in darkness and tried to think.

If he hadn't come up the trail, *if* the picture hadn't been trampled in a stompede, *if* they'd gone to Abilene instead of Sundust; everything would be all right.

Life is a roulette wheel. What'm I going to do? His head hurt. Thunder reverberated outside. A waitress walked past. "Miss!"

She turned in his direction, squinted. "I din't see you in here. Who you hidin' from, cowboy?"

He placed the empty glass on her tray. "Whiskey."

He knew why Marie was cruel to her husband. She still loved him, John Stone, and would never be happy with another man. It was the same way with him. They needed each other.

What about Cassandra? She was a wonderful and beautiful woman. It was confusing. He had no idea of what to do. *Maybe I should shoot myself and get it over with.*

He was haunted by Marie, the war, men he'd killed, friends who'd fallen in battle, his father, his mother, the Gypsy's curse, it went on and on. There was no escape from his mind, except through whiskey. The waitress placed another glass on the table. "Bring me a double, next time you pass this way."

"Ain't you lonely back here? I'll send you somebody keep you company."

"Want to be alone."

"Got just the gal fer you."

Stone sipped his whiskey. He spotted Rooney in the swirling clouds of tobacco smoke near the bar. Stone scratched a match on the table and lit the candle.

"Thought I'd find you in one of these pigstys," Rooney said. "You all right?"

"Marie is at Fort Hays, married to the provost marshal."

There was silence between them for a few moments. "What're you going to do?" Rooney asked.

"Haven't decided," Stone replied. "Wish somebody'd shoot me and put me out of my misery."

Frank Quarternight opened his eyes, Smith & Wesson in hand. It was dark, breeze ruffled the curtains. He rolled out of bed and walked to the window. The hour between supper and hard drinking. John Stone would be in one of those saloons with the rest of the cowboys.

Quarternight had supper in the dining room of the Majestic Hotel, looking out the window at State Street. Doomed to loneliness, never had a friend, didn't know how to get one. John Stone killed his brother, only family he had. Stupid goddamn cowboy wouldn't know what hit him. There'd be no gentlemanly walk to the outskirts of town this time. Brace John Stone and shoot him down.

• • •

John Stone leaned across the table, the left corner of his mouth turned down. "If you were me," he said to Rooney, "what would you do?"

Rooney was wilted, tie loosened and top button of his shirt undone. A half bottle of whiskey stood between them.

"I'd marry Cassandra without even thinking about it," Rooney said. "I want a woman who can do something more than look pretty. That's Cassandra."

"Marie was just a kid when you met her," Stone said. "Now she's grown like Cassandra. Maybe she can handle anything too."

Rooney placed his elbows on the table and looked Stone in the eye. "Marie was a spoiled brat."

"She lost her patience at times, I admit it. When you're that pretty, you spend most of your life fighting off men."

"She got awfully mad at you too."

"High-spirited, that's all. Wouldn't want one that didn't have some fight."

Marie had always been a difficult person, Stone admitted to himself. A man tries to explain these things, but it's hot air. He took her picture out of his pocket. A few days away. If she didn't want him, he'd move on. For all he knew, she prayed every night he'd show up. Now at last he'd get some answers.

"You've got to give up the past," Rooney said, slurring the words. "Throw that picture away and forget Marie."

"Got to see her."

"She's married to another man."

"They don't get along, and maybe I'm the reason."

"She forgot you long ago."

Stone didn't think Marie could forget him any more than he could forget her.

"My God," said Rooney, a note of awe in his voice.

Cassandra approached the table, and at first Stone didn't recognize her. She wore a long flowing brown skirt with a white blouse that buttoned up to her neck, a civilized woman instead of a she-creature of the plains.

"You're drunk," she said to Stone.

"Only had a few."

She sat next to him, a cross expression on her face. "I guess this is the last big toot you were telling me about."

He was a grown man, and if he wanted to get drunk it was his business. Sullenly he reached for the glass. Cassandra knew he was defying her. One moment he was a wonderful man, the next a nasty child.

"You look marvelous," Rooney said to her. "What a transformation. If you and Johnny weren't going to tie the hitch, I'd be tempted to ask for your hand myself."

Both were glassy-eyed, movements imprecise, tongues thick. Stone stared into his glass. His brain rattled in his head.

Cassandra said to Rooney, "I've promised to throw a big party for the men. Do you think I could rent one of these saloons?"

"The Majestic Hotel might let you use the dining room, it's closed at night. You could hire guitar players and fiddlers. I'll be the bartender."

She looked at John Stone slouched in his chair. Sometimes she loved him, sometimes she didn't. If Truscott had lived, no telling what might've happened. Truscott knew what he was about.

Her eyes met John Stone's, he glanced away. Defiantly he refilled his glass.

"See you boys later," she said.

She arose from the table. A few cowboys tried to talk with her. She ignored them, pushed open the batwing doors, and was gone.

Frank Quarternight stood on the veranda of the Majestic Hotel, looked down the street. It was saloon after saloon all the way to the prairie. He heard music, laughter, a hoot. John Stone was out there.

The only thing to do was work his way up one side of the street and down the other. Sooner or later he'd find him. He wore his serape over the hook, and moved toward the first saloon. An attractive blond woman in a brown skirt approached. *Short men with potbellies never get women like that,* he thought. His eyes undressed her as she drew closer. She didn't even notice him. He walked past her and entered the Sagebrush Saloon. It was the middle of the evening, and a crowd spread before him. An old man with a white goatee plunked the piano. Quarternight made his way to the bar.

"Triangle Spur in here?" he asked the bartender.

"Can't keep track of 'em all, mister. What's yer pleasure?"

Frank Quarternight placed his hook on the bar. "I'm looking for a man name of John Stone. Ever hear of 'im?"

The bartender stared at the hook. "No, sir."

Quarternight dropped a ten-dollar gold piece on the table. "I need somebody to find 'im for me."

The bartender's hand covered the coin. "I know just the man."

"Whiskey," Quarternight said.

The bartender poured the drink. Quarternight picked it up and turned around. His hook was clearly visible, and several men knew who he was. His name passed from lips to ears, and the word spread through the saloons. Frank Quarternight was in town, and somebody was going to die.

Blasingame and Buckalew sat in the darkness. Music from saloons in the distance came to their ears, and occasionally they heard a woman laugh. Blasingame was nervous, hiding like an animal in a town that once had been his. "Damn," he said.

"What's wrong, Dad?"

"Should've stood my ground. They wouldn't dare lock up their old parson. I've married a good many of the people in this town, christened their babies. They had faith in me, but I lost faith in myself."

"What about the schoolmarm?"

"Ah . . . I'd . . ." Blasingame's voice trailed off. A murdered schoolmarm in the root cellar can never be explained away.

Slipchuck arrived in town to buy supplies for the chuck wagon, but the stores were closed. The only thing to do was head for the nearest saloon and cogitate over what to do next.

He stepped on the rail, raised his bony finger in the air. The bartender filled the glass. Whores wall to wall. Slipchuck looked them over with the eyes of a veteran connoisseur. Tomorrow at this time he'd have three months back pay, and the first thing he wanted was a fat whore.

Fattest he could find. His skin was wrinkling and bones getting brittle, but a fat woman would warm his thinning blood and make him feel young again, give him something to think about during cold dark nights on the prairie.

"Hey, mister?"

Slipchuck saw a man about his age with sorrowful eyes and sloping shoulders. He looked like a pile of rags hanging on a nail. "What's on yer mind?" Slipchuck asked, hand near his gun.

"You know a galoot name of John Stone?"

Slipchuck stared at him. "Who wants to know?"

"My name's Ledbetter. Old friend of his is a-lookin' fer him."

"Rooney?"

"Yeah, believe that was his name, Rooney."

"I'm his pard," Slipchuck said proudly, hitching up his belt, "and I'm a-lookin' fer him too. We'll find 'im together, after I finish this glass of whiskey."

"You'd better let me look at that bandage," Cassandra told Don Emilio.

He barked orders in Spanish to his vaqueros, and they left the parlor. She gathered the scissors and bandages, while he sat on the sofa, pulling apart Rooney's robe, showing the bandage on his thigh.

She kneeled between his legs and stripped away the old bandage. The wound was an ugly bloody mouth on a hairy muscular leg. She dipped the washcloth into the basin, wrung it out, touched it to his skin.

Her hair was spun gold, once he'd seen her bathe naked in a Texas stream. He wanted to take her into his arms. "How is your gringo tonight?" he asked, sarcasm and jealousy in his voice. "Drunk yet?"

"Yes," she admitted.

"He knows it hurts you, but does he care? You see how much he loves you?"

She looked at his naked hairy leg, raised her face to see black mustache, white teeth, big brown eyes.

"Señora, you know what we should do right now?"

She felt a strange tingle at the base of her spine. Maintaining her composure, she adjusted the bandage carefully on the wound.

"Señora, we are alone. Think with your heart, instead of your mind."

"Be still, or it'll hurt."

She tied the bandage, felt his animal heat, last night she slept with John Stone, what was happening to her? A woman couldn't feel this way about two men. She tightened the knot, looked at him thoughtfully.

He wanted to place his arms around her, but couldn't stand. "Señora, listen carefully. I have owned many ranches, and am skilled with cattle. John Stone, he knows little about cattle. You made him trail boss because he knows how to fight, and I admit he was good when the bullets were flying. I could never take that away from him. Tonight he saved my life, and I would do the same for him. But he does not know cattle, and he does not love you. John Stone is a lost little boy. You can see it on his face. He is not for you." He placed a hand on his heart. "I will be your slave forever."

"You want a Mexican señorita, not me. No man'll ever tell me where I can't go."

He looked at her for a few moments, and her skin was gold as her hair in the light of the lantern. He swallowed hard and said, "My men will laugh at me, but you win. If you want to go to any disgusting place, even a stupid and filthy hootchy-kootchy dance, I will not stop you, but I will insist on my right to go with you, as your husband and protector."

The robe was opened nearly to his waist. If she married a Mexican vaquero, she'd say good-bye forever to the world she'd grown up in. Her mother would turn over in her grave. But he was a rancher, and an intelligent man. Mexicans are descendants of Spaniards, a great culture. He certainly knows cattle. Even Truscott thought so.

Slipchuck walked into the Peacock Saloon, stood on his tip-toes, looked around. In a corner, with a bottle in the middle of the table, sat John Stone. "There he is right there," Slipchuck said to the man who was looking for his pard.

"Which one?"

"The big gent with the Confederate cavalry hat. I'll interduce you to him."

Slipchuck threaded his way among tables crowded with cowboys, freighters, whores, gamblers, the lost, the found, men sleeping in their drool. He came to the table and placed his hand on John Stone's shoulder. "Johnny, this feller here wants to palaver with you."

John Stone turned around, saw vacant space.

"Where'd he go?" Slipchuck asked. "He was here just a few minutes ago." He removed his hat and scratched the few remaining hairs on the top of his head.

"What're you doing here?" Stone asked. "You're supposed to be with the herd."

"Ephraim sent me in fer supplies. Where's Cassandra?" Slipchuck looked at the bottle of whiskey.

"Help yourself."

There were no extra glasses on the table. Slipchuck walked to the bar and picked a glass from the rows sitting upside down on the wet towel. He heard somebody mention the name "Frank Quarternight" and it rang a bell in his mind, but lots of bells rang in those old caverns, and he couldn't make sense of half of them.

Ledbetter was a drunkard, a bum, his rags stank, and he'd been kicked in the head by a horse. His boots were worn to the bare soles of his feet, which was why he walked gingerly into the saloon. The famous gunfighter stood at the bar, his hook shining in the light of lanterns suspended from the ceiling.

"Mr. Quarternight," he said softly. "I found yer man."

Quarternight's eyes darted to him. "Are you sure?"

The messenger of death nodded solemnly.

The floor shook beneath Stone's chair, as if a giant were walking toward him. He turned and saw Koussivitsky, attired in his new cowboy clothes.

"I thought you're supposed to be with the herd," Stone told him.

"Boss lady let me stay in town, because I have business with the carnival. Tomorrow I work at the pens, but tonight . . ." He snapped his fingers. "Woman, bring me a glass." Then he sat next to John Stone and twirled his long mustache. "You look sick, my friend. What is wrong?"

"Women," said Slipchuck on the other side of the table. "They'll do it every time."

"Pah!" said Koussivitsky. "I am here in this strange land because of a woman!"

"I thought," Stone said, "you were here because you massacred a village."

"That is true, but a woman was behind it. We were supposed to be married, and then, two weeks before the wedding, she said *nyet*. She did not give reason, and left for Saint Petersburg next morning. I was so unhappy I wanted to die. Every day I think of shooting myself. She have such big breasts. I pointed the gun to my head many times. And then came the rebellion in Prozhny. I was ordered to put it down, and I was so mad, well . . . I destroyed entire village because of a woman."

Quarternight entered the Peacock Saloon. In a corner, behind a table of gamblers, he saw the grinning skull face of the dead girl.

Everyone stared at Quarternight. Chairs scraped against the floor, jackpots were scooped up, men got out of the way. Ledbetter basked in the radiance of the great man. "There he is, the big galoot in the corner to the right, wearin' the old Confederate Army hat."

Quarternight dropped coins into his hand. Ledbetter fled like Judas to the dark shadows. Quarternight looked at Stone, and Stone's back was to the door, the stupid bastard.

It grew silent in the saloon. Stone turned around, saw a man with sloping shoulders and a big belly walking toward him.

"John Stone?" Quarternight asked.

"Who wants to know?"

"Frank Quarternight."

Stone knew the name from somewhere. "What can I do for you?"

There was silence for a few moments. "My brother was Dave Quarternight, and you killed him. On yer feet, you son of a bitch. Yer time has come."

Stone felt like a ton of iron, so drunk he could barely see. Rooney stepped forward, and Quarternight fast-drew on him. "Hold it right there. Everybody back. This is between John Stone and me."

Stone dragged himself to his feet, pulled up his pants, tried to focus on the gunfighter in front of him. He always knew it'd happen someday, he'd be too drunk to defend himself.

Rooney raised his hand in a gesture of peace. "This man's in no condition to fight. Sit down and have a drink on me, my friend. Let's talk this out like reasonable men."

"Step back," Quarternight said, "or I'll shoot you where you stand."

Stone tried to clear his mind. He didn't want anybody to fight his battles. "I can take care of myself," he muttered drunkenly. "Rooney—get the hell away from here."

Rooney moved into the line of fire and went for his gun. Quarternight pulled his trigger, the saloon thundered with the shot. Rooney rocked on his heels, blood spreading over his white shirt. Quarternight turned his gun toward Stone, and Stone realized he was going to die. He recalled the Gypsy's curse, grit his teeth for the impact of the bullet.

Another shot resounded through the saloon. Quarternight was hit before he could fire at John Stone. The bullet surprised Quarternight, his eyebrows furrowed, he turned toward his assailant, trying to hold his gun level.

An old gray-bearded man drew another bead on him. Slipchuck's gun spoke again, and Quarternight was thrown against the tables, bleeding through two holes in his torso. It never occurred to him that the decrepit geezer would challenge from his blind side. He took two steps backward, fell to the seat of his pants. The dead girl knelt before him and kissed his lips. He sagged to the floor, darkness fell over him. Frank Quarternight had fought his last duel. It was silent in the saloon. Slipchuck holstered his gun. "Somebody call the doc."

Stone gazed at Rooney lying on the floor in a widening pool of blood. Rooney's eyes fluttered. At West Point it was drilled into their heads from the moment they arrived: you'd die for each other, and there was no question about it.

Guilt tore Stone's heart apart. He got to his feet, stumbled toward the table, reached for the bottle of whiskey, snatched it up, pulled the cork, raised it to his mouth.

His hand shook. If he drank that whiskey, it'd be the end of him. The genie in the bottle sang her siren song. Stone screamed like a wounded animal and threw the bottle against the wall. It shattered, whiskey flew in all directions. He turned toward the back door of the saloon.

"That old fart shot Frank Quarternight!"

Stone opened the back door, nearly fell on his face. The cool night air hit him, and he thought of Rooney dying on the floor. He dropped to his knees. "What have I done!"

In a mad frenzy he pulled out his gun and pointed it at his head. His finger tightened around the trigger, but somehow, of all possible memories to assault his mind, he remembered the parade ground at West Point. He'd marched alongside Ashley Tredegar, Beauregard Talbott, Lewton Rooney, Judson Kilpatrick, John Pelham, Fanny Custer, George Watts, and all the rest of them. He couldn't betray them. What would Marie think when she found out he blew his brains out behind a saloon?

He looked at the sky, saw Orion the warrior with his belt and sword of stars. A great merciful cloud of blackness swept over Stone. He fell on his face next to the privy, out cold.

The gold gleamed in the darkness. Blasingame ran his fingers through it, raised his hands in the air, let the coins fall back to the pile. Gold was a magic substance, a mineral alive. No lantern burned, but a light shone from the depths of the gold. It could buy an army of rampaging bastards who'd wipe Sundust off the face of the earth.

He heard three short knocks and three long ones, closed the saddlebags, threw them over his shoulder, opened the door a crack. Buckalew stood there, holding the reins of two horses, one of which was his, the other stolen only five minutes ago from the hitching rail in front of the Brazos Saloon.

Blasingame climbed onto the saddle of the stolen horse. He looked back over his shoulder at the ramshackle little cowtown on the edge of nowhere. Tomorrow night you won't exist.

The ex-pastor of the Mount Zion Church of God followed his son out of town. Blasingame had arrived with nothing but his Bible and faith in his God-given mission, and was leaving with a bag of gold. He'd been unable to find ten good men in Sundust, and God would rain fire on it, sweep the town from the face of the earth.

Something told Reverend Blasingame not to turn around and look at Sundust, otherwise he'd turn into a pillar of salt. It was like a message from God, and frightened him. He didn't look back once in his saddle for the remainder of the night.

10

STONE AWAKENED IN a hotel room. Beside him, Captain Koussivitsky sprawled on his back, his great mouth hanging open. What happened?

He remembered Lew Rooney getting shot, felt a sudden painful wave of remorse. He sat on the edge of the bed and pulled on his boots. Nearby on the floor slept Slipchuck, the man who shot Frank Quarternight.

It was early morning, stores open for business, riders and wagons in the street. Stone's stomach was in knots, head ballooned with memories of Rooney. He didn't know if his friend was alive or dead.

He walked toward Rooney's house. *I've been weak, let myself go. A man can't cause other people to get shot.* He squared his shoulders and sucked in his stomach. His backbone was straight as the day he'd marched beneath the flags at West Point. From now on he'd be a man, not a drunkard. He'd live by his officers' code, though he wasn't an officer anymore.

Thirst sucked his mouth, his confidence was shaken. What difference would one little drink make? But it never ended with just one, he knew that now. Stop altogether or become a drunkard for life.

He came to the house, knocked on the door. It was opened by sleepy-eyed Pedro.

"Is he dead?" Stone asked.

"Not yet. The doctor is upstairs with him."

Stone climbed the stairs. The door to the bedroom was open. Against the far wall, the doctor bent over Rooney's chest, the wound stitched together into a thick maroon scab. Cassandra watched from the foot of the bed.

"How is he?" Stone asked.

"Touch and go," Dr. Wimberly said.

Rooney was pale, eyes closed, tinged with blue. Anguish welled up inside Stone. He craved whiskey.

"All we can do is wait it out," the doctor said. "If he comes to, send for me."

He bandaged the wound. Cassandra and Stone looked at each other wordlessly. Stone felt like crawling under the rug. The doctor left the bedroom. Stone couldn't look Cassandra in the eye.

"Don't blame it on yourself," she said. "You can't help being what you are, and it's not your fault there's no law and order in these towns."

"I'll never drink another drop of whiskey in my life."

"Don't make promises you can't keep."

There was something he had to tell her, and this was as good a time as any. He took the picture of Marie out of his shirt pocket. "She's at Fort Hays, and that's where I'm going soon as I get paid."

Cassandra let the words sink in for several seconds, then she said, "I knew you'd leave me if she ever showed up."

"She's married to somebody else. I have to see her, find out what happened."

"I hope she really is at Fort Hays, and she throws you out on your ass!"

She left the room. The clock ticked on the dresser. The herd would soon arrive at the pens. He had to be trail boss of the Triangle Spur for the last time. His world was falling apart again, but whiskey could put it back together. "You've got to pull through," he said to Rooney's comatose form. "I couldn't handle it if you don't."

Stone descended the stairs, exploded out the front door, headed toward the stable. Maybe work would take his mind off the demons raking their claws across his brain.

Men sat on the front porch of the Bar Z Ranch, and one rose abruptly. "Look who's comin'," he said.

They gazed at two riders approaching from the direction of Sundust, Phineas Blasingame and Tod Buckalew. "This is it," Buckalew said, placing his palm near the butt of his gun.

"Let me do the talking," Blasingame replied.

Blasingame sat on his horse like a ball of clothes wearing a cowboy hat, his saddlebags filled with gold. He and his son stopped in front of the hitching rail as men crowded onto the veranda.

Some wore bandages, all were armed. Runge was in their midst, smiling weirdly. Blasingame climbed to the ground, threw the saddlebags over his shoulder, pulled his hat low over his eyes. He waited for Buckalew to join him, together they advanced toward the veranda.

"Look who's here," Runge said with a nervous smile. "The man with a bad wing."

Buckalew raised his right hand and showed the bandage. " 'S bad all right, but it ain't the only wing I got, if you're lookin' fer lead."

Runge made the brave smile he used whenever pressed. Blasingame could see gunplay brewing, but had to hold them together. He took the saddlebags off his shoulder, opened the flaps, poured the gold coins onto the ground.

The magic substance shone brightly in the sun. "Providence brought me to you for one last purpose," he said. "Sundust must be destroyed. Tonight we'll put it to the torch!"

"He's gone plumb loco," somebody said.

Blasingame dropped to his knees in front of them, filled his hands with gold, raised the coins into the air. "There's lots more in Sundust, my friends. It's waiting for us, and all we have to do is go in and get it."

"Men died last time we went in," said Runge. "That town is tough."

"Not at three o'clock in the morning when they're asleep," Blasingame replied. "Bring men in from all the farms and ranches, fifty of us or more. Hit that town like a hurricane, and when we're finished, there won't be anybody left."

"Man wants to wipe out Sundust," said a voice in amused disbelief. Somebody laughed. Buckalew saw dismay on his father's face.

Buckalew stepped forward, hand near his gun. The boys settled down. Blasingame pulled himself together for another try. "What's the matter with you men?" he asked. "I thought you were professional gunfighters. You're not afraid, are you? A few bullets flew, you lost your nerve?"

Runge stepped forward, his left shoulder twitched. "We lost six men."

"You haven't been hired to serve tea." Reverend Blasingame pointed to the pile of gold on the ground. "You want your pockets full of that, you follow me. I'll give you enough to make you rich, and the devil take the hindmost!"

They were laughing aloud now, and Blasingame's voice choked in his throat. Buckalew stepped forward, wound tighter than a spring. The men stifled their mirth. Nobody wanted to mess with him.

Except Runge, who'd always hated Buckalew. Runge moved forward and held his right hand above his gun. "You tryin' to scare somebody, Buckalew?"

"Git back with the others, or I'll shoot yer damn lights out."

The short, wiry gunfighter made his most sinister smile. On the veranda, men jumped over the rails to get out of the line of fire. Runge turned to Blasingame. "Did you tell 'im what you told me? I'm the new boss?"

"That's a lie!" Blasingame said.

Buckalew waved his father out of the way. The two young gunfighters faced each other across the lawn in front of the ranch house. A horse whinnied in the corral.

"Make yer play," Buckalew said to Runge.

Runge worked his shoulders and limbered his fingers. He maintained his thin smile, and looked like a rattlesnake in a cowboy hat. "Make your'n."

Buckalew went for his gun, and so did Runge. Both men fired at nearly the same instant, and a red dot appeared in the middle of Runge's forehead. His eyes closed and he staggered to the side, blood trickling down the bridge of his nose, then he collapsed onto the dirt. Buckalew stood still for a few moments, the barrel of his gun sending up a thin trail of black smoke.

"We don't want no trouble, Buckalew," one of the boys said, wearing chin whiskers, "but we don't feel like takin' on no whole town. That's one wild crowd of cowboys down there. I ain't never seen a man pick up lit dynamite before."

It was like his father said: they'd run if a few of them got hit. "Anybody who wants to leave, git the hell out of here!"

They headed for the stable. Blasingame and Buckalew were left alone in front of the ranch. "Don't worry," Buckalew said, placing his hand on his father's shoulder. "We'll just go someplace and start over again."

"No we won't boy."

"We can't take on the whole town by ourselves!"

"You've got a score to settle with that fellow who shot you in the hand, haven't you?"

"John Stone in town?"

"Him and his whole outfit. You said you were faster'n him, didn't you?"

"Damn right I am."

Blasingame adjusted the scarf so that it covered his face, and pulled his wide-brimmed hat low over his eyes. "No one'll recognize me."

The boys rode out of the barn and headed in separate directions, singly or in small groups, to other towns where fast hands could be bought and sold. Blasingame felt his power slip away.

Buckalew looked at him. "Runge was lyin' when he said you made him boss, wasn't he?"

"He was just trying to rile you, and it worked. You'd better pull yourself together, boy, you want to face off with John Stone."

"Don't you worry none about me," Buckalew said. "He's a dumb cowboy who got lucky. Next time *I'll* take *him* by surprise."

Blasingame scooped the gold into the saddlebags, and Buckalew looked at Runge, confidence renewed by the kill. He still had the touch, maybe even faster with his left hand. He yanked the gun, twirled it around, tossed it into the air, caught it behind his back, brought it around, and took aim. Every movement was perfect, the routine lasted only seconds.

He remembered the day John Stone humiliated him. *Your time has come, you son of a bitch. I'll feed you to the hogs.*

The railroad engine huffed and chugged clouds of gray smoke into the air. Behind it snaked cars full of mooing, hooting cattle stacked together for the last ride of their lives. They smelled acrid smoke, heard terrible scrunching sounds, moved faster than ever before. They wondered where the longhorn god was taking them.

At the end of the train, sandwiched between the mail car and the caboose, were three passenger cars, and one had a lounge with a bar and tables. The train came to a stop in front of the station, it was time to take on passengers for the run to Kansas City.

The train would leave in a half hour, but Mrs. Salter was ready with the major because she didn't want to miss it. The thought of another day in Sundust was almost too horrible to bear.

A group of citizens talked with her husband, thanking him for his help in quelling the riot, while she fidgeted with the luggage, wondering if she remembered her comb and the dressing gown behind the closet door.

She became aware of a woman standing next to her. "You look like somebody I know," Mrs. Salter said.

"Marie Scanlon?" Cassandra asked.

"Are you a relation?"

"We just happen to look alike. I realize you're in a hurry, but I've often wondered about this woman who resembles me so much."

"Don't ever let your husband alone with her," Mrs. Salter said. "She's a flirt, takes advantage of men. Most people treat their dogs better'n she treats her husband. Marie Scanlon's a dirty little two-face who'd stab you in the back. If I were you, I'd stay away from her. And if John Stone's got any sense, he will too."

Stone took off his hat and wiped his forehead with the back of his sleeve. He was seated atop Tomahawk, herding cattle into the pens.

The men shouted, whacked animals with lariats, kicked them with their boots. Dust and manure were strong in the air, Stone's nose and mouth covered with his bandanna. He looked like an outlaw, and so did the other cowboys and vaqueros from the Triangle Spur.

They rode back and forth energetically, working the cattle. The sooner they penned the herd, the sooner they'd hit the saloons, and Sundust would never be the same again.

The train whistle blew, they raised their eyes from the cattle. In the distance a train pulled out of the station, headed north toward civilization, and every man wished he were on it. With a hundred dollars in his pocket, even the lowest waddie can be king for a day.

Stone was flanked by cowboys and vaqueros, and they herded the longhorns toward the gates. The men had been working them most of the day, and only a few hundred head were left. They laughed as they rode back and forth, minds turbulent with images of drunken orgies and swarms of whores.

Stone wondered how could he hold off when everybody else was drinking. He'd given up whiskey many times, but surrendered easily at first opportunity. He couldn't do it again and call himself a man. *If I swallow one drop, it'll be the end of me.*

11

SUNDUST WAS A dot of light in the midst of a vast prairie night. Cowboys rode down the middle of the street, firing guns into the air. Groups gathered in the alleys, shooting dice. A cockfight was being held near the carnival. Saloons were ablaze with light, and men's laughter carried over the rooftops.

But nowhere was the decor brighter and livelier than the dining room of the Majestic Hotel. Half the tables had been cleared away for a dance floor, and an orchestra of two fiddles, a tambourine, and the Prairie Troubadours had been hired for the night. They strummed and hummed in practice while Slipchuck set up the bar at the other end of the room.

Cassandra spent most of the afternoon rounding up women. It hadn't been cheap, but nothing was too good for her men. They'd brought her herd to Kansas, fighting injuns, rustlers, and the elements every step of the way. Tomorrow she'd pay off creditors, but her men came first.

She knew about cowboys and vaqueros, living with them on the drive. Their main interest in life was whores. If that's what they wanted, by God she'd give it to them.

But it bothered her. Prostitution was a blot on the face of civilization, yet her men put their lives on the line for her on many occasions. She could be righteous about her life, but not theirs. They wanted a party, she'd give them the best money could buy.

She looked around the room to make certain every detail was ready, her long red velvet dress swirled in the air. It buttoned to her throat, and the shoulders puffed out. Colored bunting hung from one wall to the other. It resembled a ballroom in New Orleans before the war.

She looked at whores with bad teeth and tobacco stains on their fingers, wearing cheap gaudy dresses and the most god-awful jewelry, perfume that made Cassandra gag. Her gun-toting and knife-wielding cowboys had talked incessantly about such women over campfires all the way up the trail. These poor soiled doves were the chief romantic interests of their lives.

Everything was ready. She moved toward the door. From the other side she heard a sound like cattle rumbling prior to a stompede. She opened up, saw them freshly shaved and newly clothed, with the flushed features of drunkards, guzzling whiskey constantly from the moment they hit town.

The band broke into a Virginia reel, and the soap-smelling cowboys and vaqueros filed politely past her, grinning like dogs. One bunch ran to the bar, the other toward the whores. Diego fired a shot at the ceiling, which Cassandra mentally added to the bill.

The former *segundo* walked woodenly into the room, his purple face a horrendous mask. He'd attracted no special attention in a town full of drunken cowboys, many half-blind and numb in their brains. The former *segundo* sat at a table and gazed blankly at the revelers.

The drive was over, Cassandra had her money at last. Many times she didn't think they'd make it. The night they'd been hit by an Osage war party, she'd nearly been trampled to death. The time the Comanche warrior nearly got her scalp while she was taking a bath. One fight after another. Disaster followed catastrophe. But they'd arrived at the railhead finally. She'd clear up her business and hit the trail for Texas day after tomorrow, rebuild the old Triangle Spur, and drive north again next year bigger and better than ever.

Truscott, wherever he was, would approve. The only life for her now was the open range far from the boundaries of the workaday world. She and her men, nothing they couldn't do. If John Stone wanted to chase a picture, that was his business. By the way, where was he?

• • •

He sat on his bed in his darkened room, smoking a cigarette, looking out the window. Somewhere out there, Marie slept with her husband. He wondered what'd happen when he hit Fort Hays. Maybe she'd tell him to go away. Or they'd run off together, as in the old days.

He couldn't forget her. She was too close, the pull too strong. Three days to Fort Hays. Then he could have it out once and for all, get all his questions answered, maybe have some peace of mind at last. If she wouldn't leave her husband, Cassandra might take him back.

Sounds of the band erupted through the floorboards of his hotel room. The party was under way. He couldn't spend the rest of his life hiding from whiskey. He was weak, but not that weak. Never again would somebody else stop a bullet meant for him.

He'd wasted enough time, smoked too many cigarettes. He got to his feet and looked at himself in the mirror. He wore a new red shirt, black britches, and his old beat-up boots, because he hadn't had time yet to order a new pair of tailor-mades. Putting on his old Confederate cavalry hat, he left the room.

The lobby was crowded with cowboys trying to bust into the dining room. Word had spread through Sundust that the boss lady of the Triangle Spur was throwing a party with free whiskey and whores. The Majestic Hotel filled, everybody carried a cup or glass to put beneath the spigot of a whiskey or beer barrel. Sloppiness set in, and the floor was awash near the beverages.

Cowboys and doves danced merrily, while the band pumped out one song after another. Somebody whooped, and the second shot of the night was fired. The former *segundo* sat in a corner, his blank eyes recording the spectacle before him.

Stone squeezed through the doorway, found himself in chaos. A woman screamed on the dance floor. A cowboy grabbed her dress and ripped it off her body. Her breasts fell out, he laughed.

She groped toward her garter belt, her bloomers showed, but she found what she was looking for: the derringer in her garter belt. She pulled it and aimed between his eyes. He stepped backward, holding out his hands, talking quickly. Somebody hit him over the head with the butt of a gun, he collapsed like an accordian. Cowboys carried him to an open window, threw him outside. Meanwhile, Slipchuck stepped onto the stage.

"I was a-wonderin'," he said, "if there's any woman here knows how to dance the Houlihan!"

A female voice shrieked, and Slipchuck jumped to the dance floor. The star-crossed couple made their way to each other. She was in her mid-fifties, had seen better days. The crowd opened up; a significant performance was about to take place. Slipchuck planted his fists on his hips and placed one foot forward. The wrinkled old dove did the same. The band played a lively Irish song, and the couple danced on their toes, kicking back and forth.

Stone smelled whiskey. If he could get through tonight, he'd get through anything. The crowd spilled into the lobby and onto the street. Cowboys, doves, railroad workers, errant husbands and wives, everybody came running. The Majestic Hotel became the center of a wild frontier bacchanal. A second band, comprised of amateur cowboy musicians, twanged on the veranda. People from the nice side of town came to see what was going on, drink-crazed cowboys and doves danced in the street.

Stone sat at a table with people he didn't know, and Cassandra pulled up a chair beside him. "I'm going back to the Triangle Spur with Don Emilio," she said. "We'll see what works out."

Stone came to life. "Don Emilio?"

"What do you care? You're going after the girl in your pocket, and I hope you find her. I've got a feeling you deserve each other."

"Maybe I'm making the biggest mistake of my life," he said, "and I'll regret it till the day I die, but I've got to see Marie."

"You love her more than me, and that's the part that hurts."

"You're running away with a man you barely know. How quickly you've gotten over me."

"You're a son of a bitch, John Stone. You promised the world, and now you're leaving for the girl in your pocket."

"You're running off with Don Emilio, don't preach to me."

He was cold sober. What woman could hope to tame him? She'd given him the best love she had, but he wanted his childhood sweetheart, the girl he left behind.

Don Emilio limped toward her, sombrero on the back of his head. She arose from her chair. Stone forced himself to look in another direction. Slipchuck danced the Houlihan with the old dove. Now there's a man who knows how to live. Bounce from one to the other.

He returned his eyes to Cassandra and Don Emilio having a conversation. Don Emilio touched her cheek, and Stone wanted to punch him. Instead he looked away. The world would be a much simpler place without women. He needed a drink. Women were driving him crazy.

Something immense came to rest beside him. He turned to Koussivitsky in a voluminous cowboy shirt, arms thicker than most men's legs. "What is wrong, my friend? Women still? I say put them all in prison. If a man wants one, he take her out. If she is good, she stays out. If she is not good, back she goes."

"Not a bad idea."

"Even worse than women," Koussivitsky continued, "is being far from Mother Russia. There is an old Cossack legend about a man who loved Mother Russia so much, he sacrificed his young wife, the person he loved most, to show devotion. Threw her into the Volga, which symbolized Mother Russia to him, and she drowned. It is a true story, they say. Be glad you have your country at least."

Stone heard the scrape of a chair, and Don Emilio sat opposite him, a thin black cigar sticking out of the corner of his mouth. "I believe you have heard the good news," he said. "*La Señora* and me, we are going back to Texas together."

"You break her heart, I'll kill you."

Don Emilio smiled. "You could not kill me on the best day of your life." He turned around and hollered something in Spanish to Domingo, who brought him a glass of whiskey. Don Emilio placed it in front of Stone. "Go ahead, *borrachín*. Take a drink. You know you will give in sooner or later."

Stone slapped the glass across the table into Don Emilio's lap. Both men got to their feet and drew guns. Stone aimed his Colt at Don Emilio's stomach, and Don Emilio's gun wasn't clear of his holster.

Don Emilio grinned good-naturedly. "My leg slowed me down, I am afraid."

"It's not your leg. I'm faster than you, and you know it. You don't treat Cassandra right, I'll track you down if I have to follow you all the way to Chihuahua."

"Do not worry about *La Señora*," Don Emilio said. "She will be far happier with me than she ever was with you."

Don Emilio left the table. Stone lit his cigarette. A dove lighted onto the chair beside him. "You from the Triangle Spur?" She pressed her body against him. "Wanna go upstairs?"

"Not now," he replied.

"I'm not yer type?" She licked his ear. "Tell me what you want, cowboy. I'll do *anything*."

Cowboys cheered as more barrels of whiskey and beer were carried into the room. Somebody fired the third shot into the ceiling. Cassandra stood with her back against the wall and watched the mad drunken orgy she'd arranged. Even Mayor McGillicuddy, Alderman Shaeffer, and Sheriff Wheatlock were there, drinking whiskey, pawing doves.

It was a madhouse, the band continued to play. Underneath a table, a cowboy and a dove looked as though they were performing an intimate act. The new barrels were opened, the fourth shot was fired at the ceiling, and splinters of wood fell on the celebrants below.

Truscott would love the party, she thought wistfully. He'd been a saloon rat and whoremonger like the rest of them. Cassandra felt a rush of emotion, as if one part of her life were ending, and another beginning. She was out of debt, a whole new wonderful world lay ahead.

Slipchuck appeared in front of her, his pants half-unbuttoned, red smudges of ladies' cosmetics on his collar, cockeyed drunk. "You said you was a-gonna give us a party, and by God, you did! Could an old galoot have the pleasure of yer next dance?"

She extended her hand, and he led her to the floor. The band played a waltz, and the gray-bearded man danced away with tall blond Cassandra.

Don Emilio watched from his table, and he was at a turning point in his life too. No more tequila, because *La Señora* didn't like it. No more señoritas with flashing eyes. But *La Señora* was the golden goddess he'd dreamed of all his life. Now that he'd won her, he was a little afraid.

Diego placed his arm around Don Emilio's shoulder. "You look unhappy, amigo. What is bothering you?"

"It is not good to marry a rich woman. She will always have something over you."

Diego winked, and slapped Don Emilio on the back. "Do not be a fool, amigo. Take her for every peso she has got!"

A fight broke out near the whiskey barrels. A man leaned out a window, vomited into the alley. Stone sat at a table with strangers, and a gambler pushed a tin cup of whiskey toward him.

"Have a drink," the gambler said.

"No thank you."

"Don't drink?"

"Not anymore."

"Life is short, and whiskey a rare pleasure."

The gambler had a black mustache and goatee, and looked like the devil as he raised the cup and poured burning liquid down his throat. Stone felt wild, wanted to rip the place apart.

The principles he'd learned at West Point were silly vainglorious pomposity, and too many men had been killed, but yet those principles had saved his miserable worthless life. He had to hold on to them, because he had nothing else.

On the dance floor, cowboys and vaqueros spun doves gaily through the burgeoning throngs. A few men could be seen passed out on the floor near the walls where they'd been rolled so no one would step on them.

A dark muscular figure entered the door: Ephraim, Negro cook from the Triangle Spur. He looked around, face immobile, out of place. Slipchuck shook his hand, pulled him toward the whiskey barrels. Ephraim didn't want to go, never drank.

Ephraim moved into the shadows, feeling uneasy among so many drunk and armed white men, but he was part of the Triangle Spur too, and a trail crew is only as good as its cook.

Cassandra took his hand, pulled him toward the dance floor. Panic came over Ephraim, sure he'd get lynched. She placed her hand on his shoulder and danced him away. Ephraim felt the noose tighten around his neck, but the word passed around, he was biscuit shooter for the Triangle Spur, and the boss lady was showing her appreciation for a job well done. The blond woman and black man twirled across the floor, making certain their bodies never, under any circumstances, touched.

Stone was glad he'd never have to look at Ephraim again. He'd seen enough of his ex-slave to last the rest of his life.

There was a shriek, a clown burst into the room. He was followed by the fat lady, who barely made it through the door, then the tattooed man, a variety of freaks, midgets, hunchbacks, the sword swallower, the tumbling Gypsies. The carnival closed for the night, and the performers joined the party.

It reminded Cassandra of a painting by Hieronymus Bosch. She was amazed at what she'd done. All it took was money and the wildest conglomeration of people in the world drawn together by destiny into one clapboard hotel in Kansas, and the party careened madly onward into the night.

Blasingame and Buckalew turned their horses onto State Street, and were surprised by the mob in front of the Majestic Hotel. It looked as though a major event were taking place.

They heard laughter, music, a shot. People danced in the street like Sodom and Gomorrah; Blasingame raised the scarf over his face. Horses and wagons were sandwiched side by side at the hitching rails. Buckalew steered into an alley, and they came out behind the buildings. They rode to the rear of the Majestic Hotel and tethered their horses to a tree. They didn't loosen cinch straps, intending to be right back.

They walked down the alley, came to the street, and moved through the crowds, looking for John Stone. Blasingame spotted members of his congregation, adjusted the scarf over his face. He was dressed like a cowboy, wore a Colt in a holster tied to his leg like a gunfighter.

"What's goin' on here?" Buckalew asked a drunken cowboy.

"Triangle Spur's throwin' a party in the Majestic Hotel. Drinks on the boss lady." The cowboy raised his glass, poured the contents down his throat.

Blasingame saw a couple lying in an alley, and it appeared as if they were . . . The mayor staggered in the middle of the street, a mug of beer in his hand, shouting drunkenly. A dove passed out cold on a bench, and a cowboy rifled her purse.

It looked like the end of the world to Blasingame; he walked beside his putative son toward the veranda of the Majestic Hotel. The front door was open, they could see dancers, revelers, clowns swirling in gay profusion.

Slipchuck stood beside the whiskey bar in the lobby, watching the dancers. *Best party of my life, whole damn county's here.* He felt something against his leg. A little person was down there, and Slipchuck thought he was one drink over the line. He dropped to one knee beside her, a midget with a bad back.

Slipchuck smiled and held out his hand. "Hello, dorlin'."

"Hi," Little Emma replied in a shy voice.

"Kin I git you sawmthin' to drank?"

"No, sir."

"Want to dance?"

"Don't know how."

"Ain't nawthin' to it. I'll show yer."

He picked her up and carried her to the floor, spinning her around. The music became louder, people laughed, she felt light as a sparrow as he swooped her through the air. She giggled, her eyes sparkling in the light of the lamps.

"You're a real good dancer," he said. "You stick with me, I'll teach you the Houlihan."

The smile vanished from her face as she focused on a short, dumpy cowboy passing through the crowd. His face was hidden by a scarf, but she'd know that walk anywhere. She twisted loose from Slipchuck's grip.

"What's the matter, dorlin'?"

She disappeared into the crowd. A nervous murmur passed like a wave through the carousers. Tod Buckalew had been spotted, and the warning was making the rounds. He had his mean face on, they moved out of his way, he passed among them like the lord of death.

He scanned faces, couldn't see John Stone. Another party was in the next room; he stepped through the doorway, dodged out of the backlight, let his eyes rove. The band stopped playing, dancers came to a halt. Everybody was afraid to move. The smell of the grave was in the air.

Stone saw him the moment he entered the room. Buckalew continued to search faces, while behind him Blasingame slipped through the doorway. Cassandra sat at a table with a Mexican's arm around her shoulders. Blasingame maneuvered for a clear shot.

Buckalew advanced into the room, and a path opened before him. "I'm lookin' for a man named John Stone!"

"Over here!"

Buckalew saw the big trail boss near the far wall. A smile came to Buckalew's lips. "Remember me?"

"Where's your tin badge?" Stone asked.

"Got somethin' better," Buckalew replied, hand near his gun. "You caught me off balance once. I swore I'd kill you, and here I am."

Buckalew went for his gun, and Stone's hand slapped the worn wood handle of his Colt, swung up quickly. Buckalew's gun was clear, he drew back his hammer, and Stone drilled him through the chest.

A cloud of gunsmoke rose into the air. Buckalew took a step backward. The gun fell out of his hands, his legs became jelly. He clasped hands to his wound, dropped to his knees, looked at Stone elongated and huge from Buckalew's low perspective. Buckalew's mind filled with confusion, he collapsed onto his face.

John Stone reloaded the empty chamber. A crowd gathered around Buckalew. Stone had shot the fastest gun in Sundust. His cold, focused fury had been a sight to behold.

A corpulent figure loomed out of the darkness, Blasingame sneaking up on Cassandra Whiteside for a head shot at close range. Eve the wicked temptress would not survive this night. He reached for his gun in the shadows.

A high-pitched scream rent the air, and a furious little creature jumped on his arm. His gun fired at the floorboards, women screamed, the crowd swarmed over Blasingame, he went down. The last thing he saw was Little Emma and her fingernails buried into his wrist.

"Let me at 'im," said Sheriff Wheatlock.

The crowd rolled off Blasingame. "It's Reverend Real Estate!"

"He killed the schoolmarm!"

"String him up!"

They grabbed him roughly by his arms and pulled him to his feet.

"Now hold on!" Wheatlock said.

The drunken crowd turned angry, Blasingame had tried to shoot the Triangle Spur boss lady in the back, and no one except the U.S. Cavalry could stop them now. They dragged the former preacher to the door, somebody whacked him in the mouth, a foot crunched his ribs. The ages of darkness descended upon him.

They pulled him outside, a rope was thrown over the branch of a cottonwood. A cowboy brought a horse. Blasingame tried desperately to gain control of the situation. "People of Sundust!" he hollered. "Your souls are in the gravest danger! Be careful what you do! The blood of Christ will be on you and your children forever! Thou shalt not kill!"

The enormity of what he'd said struck him, because he'd killed too. But he'd done it for the Lord. Why was this happening? He became frightened and uncertain; they led the horse to the noose dangling in the breeze. His chest felt tight, he was lifted to the saddle, the noose adjusted to his neck. He saw fires, a sea of molten lava rolled toward him. *Thou shalt not kill. I am the handmaiden of God.*

Somebody whipped the horse's flanks, the beast leapt forward. Blasingame shrieked as the noose tightened, and his little legs kicked in the air. The molten lava rolled over his head, and his brains roasted till the end of time.

Stone lit the lamp next to Rooney's bed. The room glowed orange, Rooney's eyes were closed, skin waxen. Stone sat on a chair. *I was a drunken pig, and he the warrior. This man saved my life.*

"That you, Johnny?" Rooney asked in a voice barely above a whisper.

"How do you feel?"

"Hurts real bad."

Stone gripped his hand. "Sorry."

"You would've . . . done it . . . for me." There was silence. Rooney tried to make himself comfortable. "How long . . . I been here?"

"A day."

"Them your saddlebags . . . I see hanging . . . on the bed-post?"

"I'm cutting out for Fort Hays."

"One of my sergeants . . . saved my life . . . at Chancellorsville. If . . ." Rooney's voice trailed off.

Stone knew what he was trying to say. Somebody saved Rooney's life at Chancellorsville, Rooney saved Stone's life in Sundust, and in some other town, on another day, maybe Stone would save the life of another old soldier.

Stone threw his saddlebags over his shoulder, descended the stairs, made his way to the stable. A man has to follow his brightest star no matter where it leads.

He found Tomahawk in the stall, threw the blanket onto his back. "We're going for a ride, boy," Stone said softly in the darkness. "Just you and me, like the old days."

He heard a voice behind him. "What about me, pard?"

Stone spun around and saw a short, spindly figure with a bedroll on one shoulder and a new wide-brimmed hat on the back of his head. "You wasn't fixin' to pull out on me, was you, pard?" Slipchuck asked.

"Afraid I was, pard. Figured you wanted to stay with the brand."

"You're gonna need somebody watch yer back," Slipchuck said, " 'cause you're the man what shot Tod Buckalew, and he was the fastest gun in these parts."

"You'll need somebody to watch your back too, because you outdrew Frank Quarternight, and he was no slouch either. If you're not worried about a jealous husband taking a potshot at you, saddle up your cayuse and let's hit the trail, pardner."

They readied their horses, climbed aboard, and rode toward the big proscenium door. Moonlight cast long shadows of buildings and trees on the ground. Stone found the North Star and headed in a northwesterly direction toward Fort Hays.

The only sounds were the snorting of horses, creak of saddles, hooves striking the ground. They advanced onto open prairie, guns loaded, rifles in scabbards, knives in boots, their path led directly through injun country.

The prairie spread before them, ghostly and mysterious in the moonlight.

IT WAS LATE afternoon when I got on my horse and rode the half mile from the house I'd built for Nora, my wife, up to the big ranch house my father and my two younger brothers still occupied. I had good news, the kind of news that does a body good, and I had taken the short run pretty fast. The two-year-old bay colt I'd been riding lately was kind of surprised when I hit him with the spurs, but he'd been lazing around the little horse trap behind my house and was grateful for the chance to stretch his legs and impress me with his speed. So we made it over the rolling plains of our ranch, the Half-Moon, in mighty good time.

I pulled up just at the front door of the big house, dropped the reins to the ground so that the colt would stand, and then made my way up on the big wooden porch, the rowels of my spurs making a *ching-ching* sound as I walked. I opened the big front door and let myself into the hall that led back to the main parts of the house.

I was Justa Williams and I was boss of all thirty thousand deeded acres of the place. I had been so since it had come my duty on the weakening of our father, Howard, through two unfortunate incidents. The first had been the early demise of our mother, which had taken it out of Howard. That had been when he'd sort of started preparing me to take over the load. I'd been a hard sixteen or a soft seventeen at the time. The next level had jumped up when he'd got nicked in the lungs

175

by a stray bullet. After that I'd had the job of boss. The place was run with my two younger brothers, Ben and Norris.

It had been a hard job but having Howard around had made the job easier. Now I had some good news for him and I meant him to take it so. So when I went clumping back toward his bedroom that was just off the office I went to yelling, "Howard! Howard!"

He'd been lying back on his daybed, and he got up at my approach and come out leaning on his cane. He said, "What the thunder!"

I said, "Old man, sit down."

I went over and poured us out a good three fingers of whiskey. I didn't even bother to water his as I was supposed to do because my news was so big. He looked on with a good deal of pleasure as I poured out the drink. He wasn't even supposed to drink whiskey, but he'd put up such a fuss that the doctor had finally given in and allowed him one well-watered whiskey a day. But Howard claimed he never could count very well and that sometimes he got mixed up and that one drink turned into four. But, hell, I couldn't blame him. Sitting around all day like he was forced to was enough to make anybody crave a drink even if it was just for something to do.

But now he seen he was going to get the straight stuff and he got a mighty big gleam in his eye. He took the glass when I handed it to him and said, "What's the occasion? Tryin' to kill me off?"

"Hell no," I said. "But a man can't make a proper toast with watered whiskey."

"That's a fact," he said. "Now what the thunder are we toasting?"

I clinked my glass with his. I said, "If all goes well you are going to be a grandfather."

"Lord A'mighty!" he said.

We said, "Luck" as was our custom and then knocked them back.

Then he set his glass down and said, "Well, I'll just be damned." He got a satisfied look on his face that I didn't reckon was all due to the whiskey. He said, "Been long enough in coming."

I said, "Hell, the way you keep me busy with this ranch's business I'm surprised I've had the time."

"Pshaw!" he said.

We stood there, kind of enjoying the moment, and then I nodded at the whiskey bottle and said, "You keep on sneaking drinks, you ain't likely to be around for the occasion."

He reared up and said, "Here now! When did I raise you to talk like that?"

I gave him a small smile and said, "Somewhere along the line." Then I set my glass down and said, "Howard, I've got to get to work. I just reckoned you'd want the news."

He said, "Guess it will be a boy?"

I give him a sarcastic look. I said, "Sure, Howard, and I've gone into the gypsy business."

Then I turned out of the house and went to looking for our foreman, Harley. It was early spring in the year of 1848, and we were coming into a swift-calf crop after an unusually mild winter. We were about to have calves dropping all over the place, and with the quality of our crossbred beef, we couldn't afford to lose a one.

On the way across the ranch yard my youngest brother, Ben, came riding up. He was on a little prancing chestnut that wouldn't stay still while he was trying to talk to me. I knew he was schooling the little filly, but I said, a little impatiently, "Ben, either ride on off and talk to me later or make that damn horse stand. I can't catch but every other word."

Ben said, mildly, "Hell, don't get agitated. I just wanted to give you a piece of news you might be interested in."

I said, "All right, what is this piece of news?"

"One of the hands drifting the Shorthorn herd got sent back to the barn to pick up some stuff for Harley. He said he seen Lew Vara heading this way."

I was standing up near his horse. The animal had been worked pretty hard, and you could take the horse smell right up your nose off him. I said, "Well, okay. So the sheriff is coming. What you reckon we ought to do, get him a cake baked?"

He give me one of his sardonic looks. Ben and I were so much alike it was awful to contemplate. Only difference between us was that I was a good deal wiser and less hotheaded and he was an even size smaller than me. He said, "I reckon he'd rather have whiskey."

I said, "I got some news for you but I ain't going to tell you now."

"What is it?"

I wasn't about to tell him he might be an uncle under such circumstances. I gave his horse a whack on the rump and said, as he went off, "Tell you this evening after work. Now get, and tell Ray Hays I want to see him later on."

He rode off, and I walked back to the ranch house thinking about Lew Vara. Lew, outside of my family, was about the best friend I'd ever had. We'd started off, however, in a kind of peculiar way to make friends. Some eight or nine years past Lew and I had had about the worst fistfight I'd ever been in. It occurred at Crook's Saloon and Cafe in Blessing, the closest town to our ranch, about seven miles away, of which we owned a good part. The fight took nearly a half an hour, and we both did our dead level best to beat the other to death. I won the fight, but unfairly. Lew had had me down on the saloon floor and was in the process of finishing me off when my groping hand found a beer mug. I smashed him over the head with it in a last-ditch effort to keep my own head on my shoulders. It sent Lew to the infirmary for quite a long stay; I'd fractured his skull. When he was partially recovered Lew sent word to me that as soon as he was able, he was coming to kill me.

But it never happened. When he was free from medical care Lew took off for the Oklahoma Territory, and I didn't hear another word from him for four years. Next time I saw him he came into that very same saloon. I was sitting at a back table when I saw him come through the door. I eased my right leg forward so as to clear my revolver for a quick draw from the holster. But Lew just came up, stuck out his hand in a friendly gesture, and said he wanted to let bygones be bygones. He offered to buy me a drink, but I had a bottle on the table so I just told him to get himself a glass and take advantage of my hospitality.

Which he did.

After that Lew became a friend of the family and was important in helping the Williams family in about three confrontations where his gun and his savvy did a good deal to turn the tide in our favor. After that we ran him against the incumbent sheriff who we'd come to dislike and no longer trust. Lew had been reluctant at first, but I'd told him that money couldn't buy poverty but it could damn well buy the sheriff's job in Matagorda County. As a result he got elected, and so far as I was concerned, he did an outstanding job of keeping the peace in his territory.

Which wasn't saying a great deal because most of the trouble he had to deal with, outside of helping us, was the occasional Saturday night drunk and the odd Main Street dogfight.

So I walked back to the main ranch house wondering what he wanted. But I also knew that if it was in my power to give, Lew could have it.

I was standing on the porch about five minutes later when he came riding up. I said, "You want to come inside or talk outside?"

He swung off his horse. He said, "Let's get inside."

"You want coffee?"

"I could stand it."

"This going to be serious?"

"Is to me."

"All right."

I led him through the house to the dining room, where we generally, as a family, sat around and talked things out. I said, looking at Lew, "Get started on it."

He wouldn't face me. "Wait until the coffee comes. We can talk then."

About then Buttercup came staggering in with a couple of cups of coffee. It didn't much make any difference about what time of day or night it was, Buttercup might or might not be staggering. He was an old hand of our father's who'd helped to develop the Half-Moon. In his day he'd been about the best horse breaker around, but time and tumbles had taken their toll. But Howard wasn't a man to forget past loyalties so he'd kept Buttercup on as a cook. His real name was Butterfield, but me and my brothers had called him Buttercup, a name he clearly despised, for as long as I could remember. He was easily the best shot with a long-range rifle I'd ever seen. He had an old .50-caliber Sharps buffalo rifle, and even with his old eyes and seemingly unsteady hands he was deadly anywhere up to five hundred yards. On more than one occasion I'd had the benefit of that seemingly ageless ability. Now he set the coffee down for us and give all the indications of making himself at home. I said, "Buttercup, go on back out in the kitchen. This is a private conversation."

I sat. I picked up my coffee cup and blew on it and then took a sip. I said, "Let me have it, Lew."

He looked plain miserable. He said, "Justa, you and your family have done me a world of good. So has the town and the county. I used to be the trash of the alley and y'all helped bring me back from nothing." He looked away. He said, "That's why this is so damn hard."

"What's so damned hard?"

But instead of answering straight out he said, "They is going to be people that don't understand. That's why I want you to have the straight of it."

I said, with a little heat, "Goddammit, Lew, if you don't tell me what's going on I'm going to stretch you out over that kitchen stove in yonder."

He'd been looking away, but now he brought his gaze back to me and said, "I've got to resign, Justa. As sheriff. And not only that, I got to quit this part of the country."

Thoughts of his past life in the Oklahoma Territory flashed through my mind, when he'd been thought an outlaw and later proved innocent. I thought maybe that old business had come up again and he was going to have to flee for his life and his freedom. I said as much.

He give me a look and then made a short bark that I reckoned he took for a laugh. He said, "Naw, you got it about as backwards as can be. It's got to do with my days in the Oklahoma Territory all right, but it ain't the law. Pretty much the opposite of it. It's the outlaw part that's coming to plague me."

It took some doing, but I finally got the whole story out of him. It seemed that the old gang he'd fallen in with in Oklahoma had got wind of his being the sheriff of Mategorda County. They thought that Lew was still the same young hellion and that they had them a bird nest on the ground, what with him being sheriff and all. They'd sent word that they'd be in town in a few days and they figured to "pick the place clean." And they expected Lew's help.

"How'd you get word?"

Lew said, "Right now they are raising hell in Galveston, but they sent the first robin of spring down to let me know to get the welcome mat rolled out. Some kid about eighteen or nineteen. Thinks he's tough."

"Where's he?"

Lew jerked his head in the general direction of Blessing. "I throwed him in jail."

I said, "You got me confused. How is you quitting going to help the situation? Looks like with no law it would be even worse."

He said, "If I ain't here maybe they won't come. I plan to send the robin back with the message I ain't the sheriff and ain't even in the country. Besides, there's plenty of good men in the county for the job that won't attract the riffraff I seem to have done." He looked down at his coffee as if he was ashamed.

I didn't know what to say for a minute. This didn't sound like the Lew Vara I knew. I understood he wasn't afraid and I understood he thought he was doing what he thought was the best for everyone concerned, but I didn't think he was thinking too straight. I said, "Lew, how many of them is there?"

He said, tiredly, "About eighteen all told. Counting the robin in the jail. But they be a bunch of rough hombres. This town ain't equipped to handle such. Not without a whole lot of folks gettin' hurt. And I won't have that. I figured on an argument from you, Justa, but I ain't going to make no battlefield out of this town. I know this bunch. Or kinds like them." Then he raised his head and give me a hard look. "So I don't want no argument out of you. I come out to tell you what was what because I care about what you might think of me. Don't make me no mind about nobody else but I wanted you to know."

I got up. I said, "Finish your coffee. I got to ride over to my house. I'll be back inside of half an hour. Then we'll go into town and look into this matter."

He said, "Dammit, Justa, I done told you I—"

"Yeah, I know what you told me. I also know it ain't really what you want to do. Now we ain't going to argue and I ain't going to try to tell you what to do, but I am going to ask you to let us look into the situation a little before you light a shuck and go tearing out of here. Now will you wait until I ride over to the house and tell Nora I'm going into town?"

He looked uncomfortable, but, after a moment, he nodded. "All right," he said. "But it ain't going to change my mind none."

I said, "Just go in and visit with Howard until I get back. He don't get much company and even as sorry as you are you're better than nothing."

That at least did make him smile a bit. He sipped at his coffee, and I took out the back door to where my horse was waiting.

Nora met me at the front door when I came into the house. She said, "Well, how did the soon-to-be grandpa take it?"

I said, "Howard? Like to have knocked the heels off his boots. I give him a straight shot of whiskey in celebration. He's so damned tickled I don't reckon he's settled down yet."

"What about the others?"

I said, kind of cautiously, "Well, wasn't nobody else around. Ben's out with the herd and Norris is in Blessing. Naturally Buttercup is drunk."

Meanwhile I was kind of edging my way back toward our bedroom. She followed me. I was at the point of strapping on my gunbelt when she came into the room. She said, "Why are you putting on that gun?"

It was my sidegun, a .42/40-caliber Colts revolver that I'd been carrying for several years. I had two of them, one that I wore and one that I carried in my saddlebags. The gun was a .40-caliber chambered weapon on a .42-caliber frame. The heavier frame gave it a nice feel in the hand with very little barrel deflection, and the .40-caliber slug was big enough to stop any thing you could hit solid. It had been good luck for me and the best proof of that was that I was alive.

I said, kind of looking away from her, "Well, I've got to go into town."

"Why do you need your gun to go into town?"

I said, "Hell, Nora, I never go into town without a gun. You know that."

"What are you going into town for?"

I said, "Norris has got some papers for me to sign."

"I thought Norris was already in town. What does he need you to sign anything for?"

I kind of blew up. I said, "Dammit, Nora, what is with all these questions? I've got business. Ain't that good enough for you?"

She give me a cool look. "Yes," she said. "I don't mess in your business. It's only when you try and lie to me. Justa, you are the worst liar in the world."

"All right," I said. "All right. Lew Vara has got some trouble. Nothing serious. I'm going to give him a hand. God knows he's helped us out enough." I could hear her maid, Juanita, banging around in the kitchen. I said, "Look, why don't you get Juanita to hitch up the buggy and you and her go up to the big house and fix us a supper. I'll be back before dark and we'll all eat together and celebrate. What about that?"

She looked at me for a long moment. I could see her thinking about all the possibilities. Finally she said, "Are you going to run a risk on the day I've told you you're going to be a father?"

"Hell no!" I said. "What do you think? I'm going in to use a little influence for Lew's sake. I ain't going to be running any risks."

She made a little motion with her hand. "Then why the gun?"

"Hell, Nora, I don't even ride out into the pasture without a gun. Will you quit plaguing me?"

It took a second, but then her smooth, young face calmed down. She said, "I'm sorry, honey. Go and help Lew if you can. Juanita and I will go up to the big house and I'll personally see to supper. You better be back."

I give her a good, loving kiss and then made my adieus, left the house, and mounted my horse and rode off.

But I rode off with a little guilt nagging at me. I swear, it is hell on a man to answer all the tugs he gets on his sleeve. He gets pulled first one way and then the other. A man damn near needs to be made out of India rubber to handle all of them. No, I wasn't riding into no danger that March day, but if we didn't do something about it, it wouldn't be long before I would be.